The Short Happy Political Life of Amos McCary
and other Short Stories

Jerry File Jr.

Forward by Jerry File Jr.

To Mom and Dad

Forward

Faulkner said, and I paraphrase, that the only thing worth writing about is the truths of the human heart in conflict with itself.

There are such conflicts in each of these stories. Life can be sloppy as we make our way through its warp and woof, the best we can:

Amos McCary, the character, is not perfect. In fact, in his own way, he's greedy, even while he is largely guileless.

There are internal struggles within characters in 'Burrito,' exacerbated by pressures of commerce bearing down on everyone.

Characters in 'Eight Hundred and Ninety-Nine Dollars' are probably typical. They may be like you. Or, your neighbor.

With a 50% plus divorce rate, the character in 'Splinter' is downright normal, as are his struggles.

The couple in 'The Tall Wooden Fence' are in love and greedy, if you will, to live their new life together. And, maybe willing to go to extraordinary measures in order to preserve it.

'Shrubs' pulls out conflicts of heart that turn into new, surprising experiences for a grown man.

'Volvos' dredges up fears of loss that evaporate as quickly as they came.

'The Sacred Hunt' lets us see through younger eyes, again. Then, reminds us of our place in the universe.

These stories are slices of life in a book you can take with you to work, the coffee shop, or on a trip.

I hope you enjoy them.

Jerry File Jr.
21 August 2011

Acknowledgments

Special thanks to my friend I made in graduate school back in '92, David Hopper. This book would not have happened without David.

Posthumous thanks to Barry Hannah. I was fortunate to study for a while under Barry. He was very, very nice to me. And, he was very unselfish with what he knew, the total volume of which wouldn't fit in a salt dome. He was a giant in a little man's body.

Very special thanks to fellow Mississippian, Steve Yarbrough. I do not feel totally worthy to talk about Steve as a fellow writer because he is so, so good. I told him one time that his character, Alan DePoyster, might be one of the best developed characters in a modern work of fiction. Steve commented on my Amos McCary story. I shall always be grateful to him for that, and for his affection toward me as a fellow writer. If you want to read very good fiction-- state of the art fiction --get Steve's Bibliography and start reading. This is particularly true if you are from Mississippi because as he nails humanity, he does it through Mississippian characters. You'll 'recognize' his place and people.

Thanks to Will Primos, fellow Mississippian and Founder and President of Primos Game Calls (http://www.primos.com) for betting that reading "The Sacred Hunt" would not be a waste of valuable time during his hunting season when he tests his company's new and proposed products. Thanks to Will for his remark about the story and for letting us use it as we see fit.

Thanks to C. Leigh McInnis. C. Leigh teaches writing at Jackson State University, Jackson, Mississippi. C. Leigh looked me in the eye one night after a reading at the Eudora Welty Commons in Jackson, Mississippi-- with other people around --and said, "Man, you 'one of the writers that when I see you gonna read, I know I can depend on you; you always bring it; you never let me down; you have never wasted my time." I shall never forget C Leigh saying that to me. It sounded like angels singing because C. Leigh knows his stuff.

Thanks to one of the the coolest, if not the coolest cat I know, Gary Hilton. He did my cover (the white background part with the mail carrier Jeep and the American flag lettering in the word POLITICAL). The spooky thing is that he had not read 'Amos' before he did it. So, his choice of picture out of at least fifteen, total, was remarkable because it is the one, the only one, that captures the arc and end of the story of Amos running for the State Senate for the Great State of Mississippi. There has never, never been a day when I did not enjoy my far ranging discussions with with GH, or when I walked away not having learned or realized something new and important about how this fallen world works: GH is a sort of renaissance man with a contemporary twist that develops as the world goes forward, accordingly. You can tell from the cover that Gary has an eye for the right design at the right time. He would be a starter on any globally selected, ad/design team.

Thanks to Chad Moorer. Chad is a fine fellow and a great editor because he knows how to improve on a writer's work while recognizing at what he is good and letting him do it.

I hope I haven't missed anyone. Surely, I have. If so, I'll mention and recognize you at readings, etc.

Table of Contents

"The Short, Happy, Political Life of Amos McCary"

Amos McCary shut the Smith's mail box with care and pressed the accelerator pedal of his mail-carrier Jeep. The small, 4-cylinder engine, just behind the narrow dash board, whirled into action.

As a rural, contract, mail carrier, Amos did not have to use an official mail Jeep like the mail carriers 45 miles away in Jackson, Mississippi. He could even use his car, with or without moving the steering wheel to the other side. But, he had been buying used-up mail carrier Jeeps from the government for 30 years and rebuilding the simple engines himself because he obsessed about being and looking official, as attested by the bone yard of mail carrier Jeeps in his backyard.

The Jeeps had only a small number of leaf springs under the suspension, so they rode like Conestoga wagons. But, Amos overlooked it over all the years because he believed it was important to be, and to look, official. Doing so was even more important than the fact x-rays of his spine showed severe, vertebral degeneration, and his legs and feet burned at night, or his feet were dead numb. Sometimes his feet were so tender and sensitive that if he stepped on one of his grand children's matchbox cars, the pain could literally throw him to the ground.

Amos painted his Jeeps the official red, white, and blue like the ones in Jackson. He did not serve in Korea or Vietnam because he could not medically qualify. The US Army would not take him, so he conjured up in his mind that carrying mail was patriotic service to his country. He even contrived that somehow, carrying U.S. Mail was striking a blow at the Kremlin.

Amos kept his hair high and tight.

The only luxury Amos allowed himself was a radio, not for music necessarily, except for a little gospel, but primarily for news and commentary. Standard issue mail Jeeps do not come with a radio. Amos bought and installed his, and to it he connected a serious, drab, military-style antenna. It was secured on he back bumper. It was so long, he bent it forward and down, and secured it at the front above the door post on the passenger's side at the top of the front windshield, beyond which it jutted one foot past the hood.

With that antenna, Amos could pick up radio stations in Jackson and Meridian, and all points in between. He knew when every local and national news and commentary show came on and how long each lasted. He would move between channels accordingly, listening to Gospel music in between, when he listened to music at all.

Amos had met Barry Goldwater in 1968 while he, Amos, was in Arizona visiting his brother who lived just east of Scotsdale. His brother had finally persuaded Amos to get someone to cover his mail route and 'come west' for a week.

Amos did, but he got antsy and left a day early. He did not want to chance someone, somehow, taking his route from under him.

He did not meet Goldwater at some fancy political event or through some powerful, mutual acquaintance. He met him at a grocery store, serendipitously, people would say. But, Amos knew in his own heart and mind that meeting Goldwater was the providential work of God, and his proprietary knowledge of this was all that mattered to Amos in his bumper-sticker way of looking at life.

Amos was standing in the meat section behind his brother as his brother picked T-bones for them to grill later at his brother's ranch house in the heat on the edge of what Amos called a desert, full of coyotes, rattle snakes, and cacti. Amos thought to himself when he was out there that *even Nathan Bedford Forrest would have had a tough go of it out here,* and that he'd sure as shootin' have ridden several horses down until they dropped from heat prostration, the dying horses being all wild-eyed and lathered, passing away in the line of duty without proper accolades, and in that barren place, far, far, from green, lush, and to Amos, even Godly, Dixie.

Amos heard commotion behind him but paid no attention, for he was looking at the T-bones, hoping his brother would choose the one he had eyed for himself because he was on vacation-- he allowed himself to think

--but not wanting to say which one he really wanted because he was not buying, and he felt like it was not his place to say. Someone tapped him on the shoulder. He turned around and it was Barry Goldwater, sure as the Texas hill country.

Amos blinked his eyes-- both eyes at the same time like someone had thrown bleach in his face. Goldwater might as well have been George Washington.

Goldwater put out his hand and Amos looked down at it. Goldwater was on TV and radio shows all the time. Amos watched and listened to him, and he secretly wanted to be like Goldwater and go up to some podium and make a speech, and run for office and win, and clean up the damn government, and run all the socialist and communist out of Washington; *Yep, 'round 'em up*, Barry made Amos feel when Amos would see him on the news with Cronkite, or Howard K. Smith, or Roger Mudd.

Barry G. was ship-shape, clipped, freshly shorn, his black glasses glittered, his shoes were jet black and spotless, his shirt blindingly white. And, he was wearing the best looking suit Amos had ever seen.

"I'm Barry Goldwater," he said, "I hope I can count on your vote."

Amos managed to shake his head, "Uh-Huh," he said, "Sure, Mr. Goldwater," he squeaked.

His brother turned around, "My God," he blurted, "Its Gold---wau'ter," his voice giving away his southern roots under the split-second stress.

"Of course it is," Amos said condescendingly.

A crowd had gathered. Being on vacation, Amos had his Kodak with him, even in the grocery. He had not wanted to leave it in the car. "Someone could steal it," he'd said to his brother as they got out of brother's 1965, 2-door, Pontiac Tempest into the stifling heat of Arizona.

"Amos," his brother said, suddenly thinking of the good-fortune of his brother having the camera, "take a picture of Mr. Goldwater and me," and he jumped beside B.G. and put his arm around him like they had grown up together and were on a fishing trip. B.G. didn't flinch because he wanted to be re-elected so he could go back to his official, Washington life. Amos snapped the picture. The flash lit up the crowd like a crime scene, sans the yellow tape.

Amos wanted a picture with Goldwater, it was his camera, but he was afraid to ask. He managed to hand the camera to his brother and step beside B.G. He kept his arms to himself, folded his hands in front, and stood there with a look like Barney Fife always had when he fell into something important. But unlike Barney, Amos did manage to hold his shoulders up and back.

Blinded by the flash and stupefied by the whole incident, Amos blurted to B.G., "I serve in the U.S. Postal Service in Mississippi," as he lamely thought at that moment, that being a Postal Worker made B. G. and him colleagues in the Fed'ral system.

B.G. was gracious. But, Amos was not a vote. So, as B.G. stepped away to shake hands with voting Arizonans, he said, in a suddenly cautious tone, "Gooood, gooood."

Amos and his brother returned to brother's house and cooked the steaks. They were good and Amos's wife asked him at about 9:30 P.M., "Amos, you OK? You're awfully quiet?"

His brother said, "We talked with Barry Goldwater today at the grocery store and Amos is still shaken like a dry Martini."

Amos frowned. He and his wife were Southern Baptist. They did not drink. Amos thought the martini expression was crass. His feelings about it showed across his face like a banner behind a plane flying the beach down in Biloxi, advertising a seafood platter at The Fisherman's Wharf.

Amos returned to Mississippi a changed man. He got the film developed. The picture of B.G. and him turned out excellently, and he was relieved. He had been afraid the picture would not come out, and no one would believe him, he thought, if he did not have the picture.

Almost mystically, the picture was his authentication, authorizing him to have and give opinions on matters of local, national, and international politics and policy.

Though his eye glasses were already similar to B.G.'s, he purchased newer, black frames just like B G's. And, he drove 45 miles to Jackson one day to McRae's Department Store on Meadowbrook Road and bought himself a black, King's Ridge suit, not as nice and Barry's Hart, Schaffner, and Marx, but close, he thought. He asked the McRae's people if he could wait for the slight alterations to the sleeves and slacks so he would not have drive the 90 miles round-trip after the alteration. They said yes.

He walked down the street to the famous Primos Northgate Restaurant and sat at one of their tables with a pressed, white, table cloth and matching, cloth napkins. He had coffee and read the Jackson Daily News. It all made him feel suddenly urbane. Reading the state capitol city's newspaper with its political content, the table cloth, the cup and saucer, and the wait staff serving as though he were important, made him cross his legs in a way he didn't at his local diner, and hold the paper up to read it as he had seen stock brokers and lawyers do before they scurried off to commerce and litigation.

A big, spotless, Lincoln with suicide doors pulled up at 11:30 AM, just as Amos was about to leave Primos to go pick up his new suit. The driver wore a Chauffeur's cap. He walked around to the back door on the passenger's side and opened the door as if for a movie star.

The 'one-armed Governor,' John Bell Williams, stepped out behind his spotless, black, Allen Edmond shoes. He and his aide-DE-camp and entourage walked close by Amos's table. Amos was mesmerized by the power they exuded as they glided by in their powerful shoes and shiny suits- the Governor's with his sleeve on his armless side tucked neatly into his coat pocket -with their stern faces as the Governor of the Great State of Mississippi made his way down to the big Primos' meeting room to make a speech to the members of the Jackson Rotary Club but looking like, as he passed by leaving a fragrant wake of Old Spice, he was, instead, on his way to negotiate a nuclear, ICBM treaty with Khrushchev himself. Amos wished he had on his new suit, and that he could have walked into the meeting hall in the entourage of the Governor.

Amos followed them with his eyes as they went by and disappeared down the hallway. As he turned his head back, he looked directly at another man sitting with a lady. Their table was in the corner. The Governor had not seen them, nor had Amos noticed them as his view had been blocked by the breakfast crowd, then dispersed, and because he had been engrossed in Jackson Daily News.

Amos instantly knew because he'd seen them both in the newspapers, that the man was Willie Morris and the lady was Ms Welty. Amos could not know but Willie was visiting from New York on Harper's business to publish a story by Ms Welty. Willie wryly commented to Amos from across the dining room, "Impo'tent, aren't they?" Before Amos could gather himself to respond, Willie went on, "I asked Ms Welty if she knows the Governor's Religious denomination. She says she is not certain, but that he has a Presbyterian face." Ms Welty gave a closed lip smile and a slight nod to Amos. Then, took another sip of her coffee.

Amos wore his new suit to church the following Sunday along with a new, white shirt, a new tie, and his old but still good, Allen Edmond Wingtips, shining like boots on a Marine. Amos was a deacon at the church, but in his suit, he looked like a preacher, or a politician.

Amos kept the picture of Goldwater and him affixed to the dash in his mail Jeep and looked at it periodically as he listened to news and commentary and thought about the issues, or 'ish-sas,' as he had begun to pronounce it like many Southern, political demagogues throughout history.

He regularly said out loud as he looked down at the picture taken in front of the meat counter in Arizona, "Barry wouldn't see it that way," to an imaginary audience in his mind at his church, the Antioch Baptist Church, filled to standing. Or, to a full dining room at Hazel's Diner over in downtown Pelahatchie at 6:45 AM in the midst of the breakfast crowd as he had seen a politician do years before.

Back then, when that candidate began speaking with booming voice, the waitresses began to move quietly like angels hovering through the patrons, and Amos and all men having breakfast slowed down eating their over-easy eggs and grits and triangles of white bread toast slathered with margarine and jam, and the collective sounds of forks and knives scraping across plates, and the noises from the kitchen, all died down to a careful, low, background noise, and the politician, with his head reared back and fedora in hand, talked boldly and his voice and energy cracked in the air and set the day off to a run like a shot of black, campfire coffee for everyone in the diner, Amos included, even though they had not been quite ready for work and action before the candidate showed up.

The story of what political and oratory acumen and skills Amos developed, happened in the confines of the Jeep, in his interactions with all the people on his route, and in his experiences through forms of leadership in the small, country, Baptist Church, and its deacons' meetings.

The microcosm of the Jeep with its Goldwater picture on the dash and its radio perpetually presenting big, national ish-sas, his deep knowledge of the people gathered over 30 years on his route and their families in their small community where everyone knew each other, and the political machinations of the small, Baptist Church and its Deacon Board-- both church and board having democratic polity, where there were always issues, lobbying, influence peddling, votes, and winners and losers --slowly molded Amos and his mind like clay on the potter's wheel to think too stupendously about himself while he simultaneously stood on a very, very small stage, a stage that deceived him into thinking he could wear a Hart and play large like the local, state, and national political figures he had observed and revered for years.

The epitome of politics inside the cab of the Jeep, in his mind, and in the quasi-political worlds in which he lived, was grossly simplistic, and predicated on a morality and an ethic that did not exist in the real, official, larger political arena where men and women politicians were gladiators, bent on sinking a proverbial ax into the skull of any and all opponents in their zero sum game, which they played right out in front of the populace, as if political life were a play.

Amos had not been on the true inside of state-wide or national politics, nor had he been allowed to even see behind the curtains. But he did not realize this, so he was blissfully ignorant of the ruthless underbelly as he blithely went about being deacon, talking national ish'sas, particularly, as he was fond or saying, "as they relate to State and local matt'as," and being Governor, or U.S. Senator, in his own mind.

Amos's wife was on him to retire from his mail route. He had been doing it for a more than 30 years. His back, legs, and feet were getting worse.

Simultaneously, many in the community began to think their local state Senator was becoming out of touch. What Amos learned through talk on the mail route was that people perceived the Senator was now acting like a big shot. And, the thing that really drew their ire, was that he recently missed an important vote during a special session of the Senate because he was at Disney World with his family.

It mattered not, as it came out later, that he had scheduled and paid for the trip a year before, and that the Senator could not have known, a year before, that the governor would call the special session that necessitated the vote. Now, the local economy was weak and people were mad at politicians. Many of his constituents had never been, nor would ever go, to Disney World.

Moreover, it came out, he had tried to get a colleague to vote for him as though he were present but the colleague was not allowed to by the Speaker when the Speaker realized it could blow back in his own face. So, the important vote was missed altogether, and the missing itself was perceived by the people to be further tainted by the shadiness of their Senator's trying to work around the rules to cast the vote that he could not make himself because his body was at Mickey's Kingdom in Florida.

The other thing Amos heard people on the route rumble about was that the current Senator was being weak on immigration-- illegal Mexicans in particular. While that was true, the Senator was no complete, political dummy. He had his own good reasons not to worry too much about immigration.

The first was that immigration was largely a Federal issue: The

Senator knew it. Amos did not.

The second reason the Senator laid off immigration had to do with the fact that the Senator, Doug Smith, was son-in-law to the owner of the local chicken plant, Dale Staples, who also happened to be Chairman of the Deacons at Antioch Baptist Church, Amos's church.

Moreover, during business hours, Dale's chicken plant had more Mexicans in it than there were spectators in the Plaza de Toros in Mexico City at the height of the bullfight season. Dale's company had buses with blacked out windows. They hauled the Mexicans into the gate of the plant in the morning, and out of the gate in the evening, to a compound of bunk houses he had on private land eight miles outside the small town on a county road. Everything the Mexican workers needed was out there at the compound, and if an item was not part of the set up, it was in the store Dale owned within walking distance. "Their money spends there like it does anywhere else," Dale often said to his son-in-law.

Dale bought his help at wholesale; then, 'sold 'em necessities at full retail.

Amos knew about the situation and strongly disagreed with it, but he was intimidated by Dale and never said anything to him or anyone else about it, except, of course to his wife when they were home. He'd get on a rant and talk about how UN-American Dale was, and his wife would let him talk until he got it out of his system.

Some people, and even some political thinkers and writers over in Jackson, began to think Senator Doug Smith could be defeated by the right candidate in the next election because Smith truly had built up some strong negatives, although no one in the district would talk about it because many livelihoods were directly or indirectly connected to Dale Staples. So, many voters secretly hoped Doug would be beaten without Doug or Dale knowing what they were thinking and how they voted.

The first person who brought up Amos running for the seat was Ms. Sigrest. "Amos," she said, "why don't you stand for that seat in the Senate? You know more about politics and such than anybody I know. We need good people like you over in Jackson."

The next was Jack Brown. JackBrown, people said both words together as a single word for as long as anyone remembered, was an Iwo Jima Marine. "Hell, Amos," he barked one day as they stood at the road by the mail-box, "some are saying you ought to run for that seat in the Senate, take out that Doug Smith and his damn daddy-in-law, I say, Hell yes, you do it." JackBrown received his retirement from the Marine Corp and had no financial ties to Dale Staples. JackBrown was a staunch Presbyterian. He told Amos, "Amos, taking action for the Kingdom is not much different than taking an island to improve civilization, except you use guns to take the island."

"Oh, JackBrown," Amos said obsequiously, "now, there is nothing wrong with Doug and his daddy-in-law."

"The hell you say," JackBrown shot back like a Browning Automatic Rifle, "they control this place out here, and it is high time for a change. Dale has that plant full of Mexicans, everybody knows it, and nobody will do anything about it."

This kept on for several months. Amos started to believe his own press.

One night over dinner as he and his wife ate meatloaf, squash from Amos's garden, and corn bread in the breakfast nook that had not been remodeled since the house was built in 1971, Amos set his fork down and leaned in with his elbows on the yellow topped, Formica table. The light from the matching swag lamp shown down on his head, creating serious shadows on his face.

Amos said, flatly, "I think I'm gonna run for the Senate. What do you think?"

"I thought you might," she said. "That's fine with me if that will get you out of that buck-board. What about Dale? How you going to handle that part of it?"

"Oh, Dale will be OK. He understands. Politics is politics."

"Politics *are* politics," she said.

"Yea, I know, that's what I said," he said.

So, approximately 30 years after he met Goldwater and had since been riding around in his Jeep, pontificating into the stale air of the cab to the crowds of people in his imagination, and in literal, small, democratic microcosms in his community and church, Amos was officially taking the plunge, for the people.

The next day he drove to the Secretary of State's office in Jackson and registered. He left there, and taking $7,000 of his own money, went to a sign company and ordered signs, push cards, bumper stickers, and lapel buttons.

Before he left Jackson, he went to McRae's Department Store in Northpark Mall in Ridgeland, and bought himself a deep blue, vaguely pinstriped, Hart, Schaffner, and Marx suit; three new, white shirts; and, three new, patriotic, American-looking ties, made by some man named Tommy Hilfiger.

"Amos is Famous for Miss'ippi" was his slogan on all his material. He'd thought about it a lot. He liked it. It *was* kinda catchy. The man at the printers made the art crisp and American-looking. Amos thought it just might win the day.

He knew the law did not allow candidate push cards in people's mailboxes with their mail unless the cards were mailed with postage, but he could honk the horn. If they were home and they could come out, he could hand them one. Or, he could take a minute, if they weren't home, go up to the house, and put a card in the screen door. He did these things, and it seemed to him that everyone on the route was genuinely happy he was running. They seemed to be behind him.

His confidence grew. He got where he could shake a man's or woman's hand profusely, look them in their eyes, and say with as much conviction as Theodore G. Bilbo had about himself, "I'm Amos McCary. I want to be *your* Senator in Jackson. Can I count on your vote?"

But, aside from Amos' escalation in confidence and the improvement in his communication skills, there was one thing he had in his favor that had never been calculated into a race for the Legislature. Doug Smith and Dale Staples did not realize it for weeks, and they likely would not have if Doug and Dale had not developed an educated hunch Amos possessed more momentum than he should.

Their suspicion prompted Dale to pay $2,500 to the Southern Institute for Political Studies for them to conduct a poll. What they learned shocked Doug and Dale: Amos had very high name recognition throughout the district, not just the part in which he lived and circulated the most; and, if the election were held the day of, or immediately around, the poling date, Amos would win by a decisive 16 points.

Doug and Dale were stumped for days. Amos was a political nobody. Sure, Doug and Dale acknowledged to each other as they drank coffee and strategized at Hazel's, that Doug had built up some pretty big negatives. And they understood that there was a certain political malaise across the state and country that naturally blew back on incumbents. But none of these could account for the outcome of the poling data.

They were missing something. What was it? For the first time ever, a challenger had them flummoxed.

"We're not accountin' for something, Doug, and I'm not sure what it is. But I aim to find out, and quick. Else, you'll loose this thing to this dumb-ass, Reagan-wanna-be-mail-carrier," Dale said, looking at Doug in complete seriousness. Doug looked back, and a cold chill shot through him. He knew his father-in-law knew more about the local and state-wide political machine, and people in general, than he did. If his daddy-in-law was nervous, he thought, *I should be wettin' my britches.*

Dale was thinking about his daughter and his grandchildren. Doug was no paragon of intellect or ambition. It was no secret in the family that Dale wished his daughter had never met and fallen for Doug at Mississippi State. Dale called him *the good looking dumb-ass,* or *Tarzan* after he met him the first time, but there was nothing Dale could do when it happened. Dale complained to his wife that as soon as that dumb gorilla got his hands all over his baby girl, she lost her connection with the reality that Doug is a walking idiot, and worse than that, she just had to go and marry him. "She...eye...T," Dale had exclaimed under his breath when he heard the nuptial news.

The wedding itself had cost Dale $25,000, a very big sum for a wedding at a small, country church, and a thing abhorrent to Dale, and with little chance of payback, save grandchildren down the line. Even grandchildren presented the risk they would turn out like their daddy instead of Dale, Dale had thought.

Nobody but the other fellow knew that Dale had even secretly talked with his life-long, best friend and fellow Mason about arranging for Doug to have the brakes go out on his car on one of the skinny two-lanes around Starkville. But, Dale said no when they realized he could never be certain his daughter would not be in the car.

And, after having two more Makers Marks over ice in front of the fire at the Masonic Lodge, Dale and his colleague in the secret world talked about deploying the favorite method of the elite: poisoning. His friend informed Dale it could be done professionally, by a real Cold War spook, for $5,000. Dale had commented he'd give $5,000 so fast it would make your head spin, but Dale never went forward to a meeting with the killer because he had seen stings on T.V. On top of the risks of the T.V. style sting, he calculated that even if he did not get caught, his daughter would know, she just would, and the risks she would withdraw from him for life were too great for him to assume.

Dale and Doug both knew as they sat in Hazel's that if Doug lost this election, all he would have to fall back on was selling accident insurance. Both knew he was not good at it.

Even Doug's selling much accident insurance depended on Dale's contacts and pressure. However, Doug did present specific value to Dale in the Legislature as a vicarious vote, and a public policy spy who doggedly looked out for Dale's many, political and business interests.

Dale kept four or five women on an adulterous string. They were either married, and they and their families were economically entwined in one or more of Dale Staple's enterprises; or, they were divorced, or widowed, and somehow dependent on Dale for a living. One of the widows was their waitress, Maggie, whom Dale had been sleeping with, off and on, for 12 years. She was financially dependent on Dale because although she did not know it, Dale was the majority, silent partner in Hazel's diner.

Maggie lived on the other side of the district. Dale had learned a long time ago that all politics really are local. "Maggie," Dale said across the empty diner since it was 3 o'clock in the afternoon. Maggie came over. "What have you seen about how Amos McCary is getting the word out over there where you live?"

"The mail carriers," she said.

"What?" he asked.

"The mail carriers," she said.

"He's mailing to the people? That's expensive."

"No," she said, "they handin' out the cards if the people 'home, or puttin' the cards on the door if they not. They doin' it all the time, over and over. I thought you knew that. I coulda told you that 'long time ago."

"We gotta go," Dale said. He got up, leaving a $5 bill on the table for $1's worth of coffee. "I'll call you later, Maggie. I want to know more about this."

"You call me," Maggie said through a private smile.

Dale went back to his office and got on the phone until 6 PM. He got back on the phone the next morning at 7:30 AM and made phone calls all day to people all over the district and in Jackson until he had it figured out. He called Doug at 6:30 PM. "Come over here to my office," he said when Doug answered the phone.

"Can I come over first thing in the morning? We've got people coming over and. . ."

Dale interrupted and barked, "I don't care if Hubert Humphrey is coming back from the dead. You get your gimp ass over here right now. I've been on the phone all day for you, you slackered, and if you want to win this thing and not have to sell burial and accident policies all your miserable life, you get your ass over here, *right now!*"

"The mail man was going to win, and we didn't even realize it," Dale said to Doug, who was sitting at the other end of the huge conference table in the luxurious, executive conference room, deep in the bowels of the clammy, chicken plant.

"You really think so, Dale?" Doug asked in stupefied tone.

"Yes, I know so. I can't tell if the guy is a sleeper and knows what he is doing, or he's like a hog who found a pile of acorns. It doesn't matter. He's done the right things straight from the get go, and he'da won if we hadn't run that pole and known the numbers. He hasn't run a pole, so I don't even think he knows how good he is right now. But I do, and we gonna stop the mail truck 'fore it runs right up our backside."

"What did he do from the beginning that was so good?"

"What do you care," Dale snapped, but then settled down to explain. "The man was a nervous public speaker without a real message, so he starts out making his talks at each and every nursing home during activity hour. And, I mean every one in the district. Especially the ones with independent and assisted living. I guess he knows they can leave and drive to the polls. So, he gets better at his talk and finds him an issue, then he starts to get himself invited to churches to chat, starting with that damn JackBrown's, Presbyterian outfit. Then, he goes to the black churches scaring the blacks about the Mexicans, and after he gets better, he's at all the grocery stores and convenience stores saying 'Hi' to the people and handing out cards and all the things *you* aren't doing. He's in the Piggly Wiggly like he owns the joint, and somehow he knows how to hover around the meat counter when there is a special on sirloins or pork chops advertised in the paper. And Hell, *I* own the Piggly Wiggly."

"How did he get into the churches?" Doug asked.

"The damn APWU members, all their churches, that's how," Dale spurted.

"What's that?" Doug said.

Dale glared and his face turned red as a sugar beet. "United Postal Workers Union you dumb-ass! His mail carrier friends have been distributing his fliers to every dang person in the district, he's spent $12,000 on signs and cards and, though I haven't looked at his disclosure yet, I know that wasn't all his money. He probably raised or was given $5,000 because I know his first order of materials was $7,000, and he almost certainly had to put that up himself. Nobody would have bet on him from the get go. Other than JackBrown and his church, all or most those carriers go to church. They got him in, maybe not in the pulpit, but you can bet they got him into the men's Sunday School, and the men told their wives, or the ladies Sunday School, and the women told their husbands, or both."

"So how we gonna beat him?" Doug said with hand-wringing in his voice.

"He screwed up picking his big issue," Dale said, "yep, it looks and sounds good, but its where he'll get beat, that is if you do exactly what I say, when I say it. If you don't, I swear I'll wring your stupid neck. This is gonna be a lot of trouble and I already have plenty to do. You better not blow it."

"Immigration is how we'll beat him?" Doug asked.

"Yes. Immigration: Just watch. There will be an article on immigration written by you coming out in the papers tomorrow, and there will be another next week, and another the following week, and another just before election day. All are being ghost written by a friend of mine in Washington. She'll first hit high, national notes the mail man doesn't know and can't handle in time. Then, she'll have it brought down to the local level right before the elections. Here are copies of the articles," Dale said as he slid a manila envelope like a hockey puck down the long, shiny table. "They are short. Read every word and memorize the arguments, positions, and all the points. Talk like she wrote, use the same words and phrases. Also, my secretary is typing you a speech; pick it up at lunch tomorrow, memorize it, and be ready," Dale said.

"When do I give it?" Doug asked.

"See, godamighty, there you go, you give it when I say give it. Have it memorized by this weekend, and I mean it. Do not screw this up, the speech will be the zinger that brings home the bacon, if you screw this up, the mail man will fry *your* bacon. I am not kidding."

The President of the local chapter of the American Postal Workers Union was a Yankee named James Shefchuk. James had moved to Mississippi from Ohio, 15 years before. He was a politician, too, else he would not have aspired to be president of the local chapter, nor would he have won. Dale knew him, but not well, but he knew he was a high ranking Mason. Dale also knew he was an avid hunter of Mississippi Whitetail deer, and that he belonged to a fine, expensive hunting club up in Lowndes County on the Tombigbee River. And, Dale knew he had tastes for Safari and big Texas hunting, but had done neither.

Dale paid him a visit in Jackson. James saw Dale's ring and lapel pin. They shook hands in the secret way.

Sitting in the man's office surrounded by four walls of Lowndes County White Tails with great antler mass, Dale got to the point.

"James, I am here to talk with you confidentially, you agree?"

"Depends," James said protecting himself but not wanting to miss any opportunity to racketeer if profitable. "What if you want to talk about something illegal?"

"I don't," Dale said.

"OK," James said, "Let's hear it, and if I don't like it, or do not want to chance being construed as a contracted party by talking about it, or if it makes me think I could ever be at risk for miss-prison, I'll stop you."

Dale said, "Well, I'm wondering about your man, Amos McCary, the one running for the state Senate."

"What about him?"

"Do you know him well since he's one of yours?"

"Amos is retired now, as you likely know. He's a good man, simple-minded, 'want to change things for the better' kinda guy, you know, but do I know him well? I just know him through periodic union gatherings he attends along with hundreds of others." James stopped, sat there, and let the room fall silent.

Dale spoke first. "Let me be blunt. I'd like him to loose, really. I'm concerned about this immigration issue he pushes so hard."

"Why Immigration?" James asked.

"Well, it takes a certain number of illegals in the work force to make the Miss'ippi economy work at its fullest. His pushing could mess up the balance that must be there."

"That's your opinion," James said. "But, what do you want me to do about Amos. I have nothing to do with him, especially since he is retired."

"Well, you do, actually," Dale said. "Particularly since he's retired...in a 'round about, but real way, yes, you do."

"How?"

"We'll talk about it, but I don't have time right now. We can talk about it in South Texas. I have a hunting preserve down there that goes to the edge of Mexico. I'm meeting some people day after tomorrow for a couple of days to do a little light work; shoot a hog; maybe some birds. Take off a couple days and go down there with us. I'm taking the Turbo-prop, back and forth won't take long. All you have to bring is you; we got plenty Browning's and Benelli's."

James sat there knowing Dale was up to no good, but being highly political and no good, himself, he was going. *Drop right into south Texas on a Turbo prop and shoot hogs and birds and eat like a king, are you kidding,* James thought.

Dale slid a card across the desk. "Here's my cell number. Also, look at that internet address on the card; that's our place down there. Airstrip is on the property. Call that Texas Congressman's office. I wrote name and number on the back. Ask for Michelle. Tell her you're my friend. Tell her I said put you through to the Congressman. He's in the office this week. I just talked with 'im. Tell her I said he is expecting your call. Ask him about me. Ask him about our place down there. Call me tomorrow and tell me you're going. Come to the Jackson International Airport at Eight AM, day after tomorrow, the private jet operation on the right 'fore you get to the big terminal. I'll show myself out."

Dale stood up, turned on a dime, and walked out of James' office.

On the way back home, Dale called the Superintendents of the school districts in Doug's Senate district. Mississippi has 83 counties and over 160 school districts; Doug's Senate District contained several school districts. Dale was the most powerful member on his school board and had very strong pull in the others. For decades, he had cultivated positions and grabbed power for such moments.

Dale called all the superintendents one by one. He duplicated the call he made to Superintendent Jim Bell to all of them, except he tailored the facts about family and situation, accordingly. "Jim, Dale Staples, how you doing? Yea, I'm fine. Look, I need to talk with you a minute. This mailman running for the Senate is pushing pretty hard, and we don't want him to win because he doesn't understand edge-a-cation in Mississippi. You need to make sure all the schools' employees and their families come out and vote for Doug."

"Well Dale, I don't know if I can do that, I mean,..."

"Jim, you might mean whatever it is you were about to say, but I don't have time to hear it. Let me be real clear what *I* mean. It will be known which candidate teachers and school employees vote for, and, if you don't get them all to vote right, you can kiss that Crown Victoria, all that gasoline, and your $90,000 yearly salary good bye. You'll have to move away to get a damn job in edge-a-cation; you hear me? Let's be real clear here; you've been blessed with that job. Everyone knows you just built..."

Jim tried to say something, "Jim, don't interrupt me. As I was saying, everyone knows you just built your big house and got a loan from Merchants Bank for $350,000, with zero down. You got two kids in school, one at Millsaps and one at Mississippi College, both private, and the cost is busting your chops. Your wife is selling a little real estate, *a little,* and you and I both know that doesn't cut it. You need to do the right thing on this." Dale hung up.

He called his second cousin's son immediately after that. If someone else had been in the car with Dale, he would not have known what Dale meant by what he said. "You going down to Baton Rouge tonight and get those South Americans, and get them back and in your barn before day light, right?" Second cousin's son responded on the other end. Dale said, "Good, that's good. 'this goes right, we'll see what Merchants and Farmers can do about the loan for those new chicken houses. See you at church Sunday." Dale hung up.

James Shefchuk called Dale. "Dale, James Shefchuk, here. I'll see you at the airport."

The articles ghost written by a professional in Washington in Doug's name started coming out in the papers as planned. Amos read the first article and had an uneasy feeling. He would remember later that he wondered why, after he'd been silent on the issue all along, Doug would come out on immigration and even write about it in state and local newspapers. Amos thought about writing an article, but he didn't have anything much to say about illegal immigration except that he was against it. He did not know the legal points Doug made in the paper, and he did not have time, or research staff.

Dale met James at the Airport. As they sat in the private aircraft waiting area, Dale said, "The Turboprop is in maintenance."

James said, "What does that mean?"

Dale said, "Well, that means we're going to have to fly the G5, I know it is shabby, but hey," he smiled.

James said, "G5 as in Gulfstream 5?"

"Yep," Dale said, "friend of mine popped in to go with us, gonna ride with him. South Texas won't even get the engines hot, but hey, somebody's gotta fly in it. 'Don't want the gaskets to rot."

James smiled. He had never flown in a G5.

Dale went to the front of the plane and called the ranch on a satellite phone. "You get the Senorita's?" he asked before hanging up. "Good, set the equipment up? Good."

They landed at the ranch and were picked up by a brace of Safari-rigged, Mercedes G-Wagons and driven to a lodge, the likes of which James had seen only in pictures.

They changed clothes and rode out to a cushy blind. James took a hog with a German made, Blaser, rifle with 7 Mag barrel as if plinking a can off a fence. "That's a sweeeeet rifle," James said.

They began sipping whiskey as soon as they returned while the help skinned the hog and put it in coolers, on dry ice, to be shipped back to James' house the next day. It was on his door step when he arrived home. They ate succulent, thick steaks, cooked perfectly, and drank wines James had only heard about.

That night, James was in bed in his own luxurious room and was so inebriated, he thought it was a dream when two stunningly beautiful women, who looked as if they stepped off a fashion runway in Paris or Buenos Aires, came into the room, dropped their robes in unison, and elegantly slipped into his bed. The expensive cameras, imbedded all over the room, captured it all as if it were daylight. James went into a deep sleep after the women left. In the morning, he was not sure the women had been real. He did not ask.

They drank Bloody Marys with breakfast. James felt more intoxicated than normal, but in a good way, he thought. He was aware that he felt uninhibited, but still together, and that he was having a good time he could only think of in terms of feeling more smooth than usual for the same amount of liquor. He had intermittent hunches of the slipping of time in a way he had never experienced. He brushed it off because he wanted to look good. Dale excused himself, saying he had to make some phone calls, and that he would meet them afield, later.

James and the others drove to the edge of Mexico. There in the field, they drank the smoothest whiskey to ever cross his lips over what seemed to be the coldest ice, ever, and they shot birds with Benelli's until his shoulder hurt. Then, some of the other men who were in the know, started to laugh and high five when two, blacked-out Suburban materialized over the tan horizon. When they arrived, young Mexican girls got out and James heard someone say, 'felacion,' and that the girls would do it to all the men right there for $5, US, each. James thought again how uninhibited he felt after drinking the mysteriously potent Bloody Marys, and the strangely powerful Whiskey. He had no resistance. He did not know about the powerful, still and movie cameras in the brush, 100 yards away.

The next, Washington produced article in Doug's name, came out in all the papers in Mississippi. And, as if out of the blue, all the state-wide political talk shows brought the article up for discussion. Even the biggest, radio talk show in Mississippi contacted Doug and invited him to come on the air. He drove over to Jackson and went into the studio. Listeners called in from all over the state. He had read and studied all the articles and the speech like Dale had instructed and he did very well on the radio; so well, that suddenly he was the State Legislature authority on the Federal aspects and State ramifications of illegal immigration.

Amos listened to the show coming down his big antennae and through the radio in his mail Jeep as he sat in it out at his barn. Doug sounded good and professional. Amos had never been on state-wide radio.

He did not know he could sound good, too.

He listened and began to understand that he had brought up the issue early, maybe too early, and that Doug was more experienced than he had realized. All Doug had to do was wait until the last minute and hook his wagon to the issue. He would be in as good a position on it as Amos; that was exactly what Doug had done. Doug was the incumbent and was better off to begin with. Voters had a short memory, and, since he'd come out strong on immigration and become the state's authority, they'd probably forgive him for Disney World, and everything else.

Amos felt he was in trouble. He had already retired from his mail route.

It started drizzling rain as Amos sat there in his mail wagon listening to Doug on the radio, running away with his core issue. Amos mustered as much a glimmer of thought as he could on the political game at hand. He had to. He had retired from his work, and the prospect of having no purpose made him feel he had to win. So, he started thinking just what Dale thought he might, and against which Dale had formulated a foil: Amos began to think in terms of a grand gambit that could swing it back his way at the last minute and win the thing. But, Amos had no idea at that moment what it could be.

Amos went to church Sunday. The deacons had a short meeting between Sunday School and the worship service about an upcoming Revival meeting. Amos went into the meeting. Dale presided and Amos and Dale and all the men shook hands, and when Amos shook Dale's hand as Dale smiled and said, "Morning, Amos," Amos had a feeling of foreboding, a feeling that he had stepped into a ring with professionals, months before, and he had no idea how to fight them. A chill went up his spine like January in Dakota.

The talk before and after church was of immigration, and of Doug on the radio, Doug in the newspapers, and that Doug might have awakened to the people's concern but that Amos had done it first. People told Amos to his face they were still for him. One of the deacon's wives, a school teacher and an Eastern Star, assured Amos she was behind him, and then she said something as if in passing and Amos asked, "What was that you just said?"

She told him that the Simmons man had illegal South Americans helping him with his chicken houses and they would be there for another month or two, depending on the work, and that as far as she knew, they lived in his barn, and they only worked at night so no one would see them and turn Simmons in.

Amos was quiet at lunch in the Cyprus nook and thought about Simmons and the illegals. "What's wrong, Amos?" his wife asked.

"Nothing," he said, "I'm just thinking."

James Shefchuk was in the den and his wife was in the kitchen making dinner, talking loudly to him though the door about the colors she wanted to paint the kitchen as he walked up and put the DVD of the hunt Dale had given him into the player. He held the remote control in his hand and stood in front of the TV for no reason, except he wanted to hurry up and see how the first day hog hunt footage came out; how he looked shooting the Blaser; how the hog on his doorstep when he returned, folded in the dirt at the crack of the rifle as if God had snatched his heart out of his chest.

The inside of his bedroom at the Lodge came on the screen and he saw himself lying there in the dark. He saw the lithe women come in. He quickly pressed stop; He almost fainting.

He threw up in his mouth.

The big arc of the whole trip swung into his mind, and he felt stupid that he had let himself be set up, *I should have known,* he thought, *it was too good.*

He went outside, washed his mouth out with water from the hose on the deck, flipped open his cell phone and dialed Dale's number, while looking to make sure his neighbor was not on his patio. Dale answered.

"This is James," he said.

"Yes, James, did you have a good time?"

"Look," James hissed.

"Whoa," Dale responded, "You must have watched the DVD, nice movie isn't it?"

"Look," James said.

"No," said Dale, "you look. I'll call you in the morning at 8:30, and I'll tell you what you are going to do, and you will do it." Dale hung up.

The next morning at 8:30, Dale called James' office. James' secretary buzzed him. He took the call. "James," Dale said, "this is simple. I want you to call Amos McCary. He will listen to you since you are the big wheel in the Union and he thinks he's Audie Murphy. Tell him you read the newspapers and heard Doug on the radio and that your political experience tells you he needs a big move, something big and high profile to take back momentum and win against Doug, and tell him he needs it now, not days from now, since the election is so soon. Tell him if he gets some sorta press on something big today or tomorrow, he might have a chance."

"Dale," James said.

"No, James," Dale said, "I know you want to talk about this movie and all that, but we're all busy trying to win this 'lection right now. Just do what I said, and anything else I say after this, and you and I will talk after the election."

James called Amos. Amos was surprised to get the attention of the president of his union. It made him feel good. He thought this might be the big gambit. The union was calling to endorse him. James told him he could not do that, but that he was calling to tell him they were all proud of him, and that there was something he would recommend. He told him exactly what Dale told him to say. Amos asked if he could come to Jackson and meet with him. James lied and said he had been called to Washington and had to fly out of Jackson in two hours.

Dale drove by James' office on his way to the U.S. Attorney's office.

He did not stop in.

Amos called the local newspaper and asked for the Editor, who was a Methodist and a Mason. Amos did not know him.

Amos did not know that Dale was the silent, majority owner of the local paper by rescuing the Editor-owner from bankruptcy years before, thus saving the paper from takeover by Gannett. The transaction had been private. Dale's name and ownership percentage were not recorded at the Secretary of State's Office. But, if someone bothered to look in the UCC filings at the office of The Secretary of State, they would find an UCC Financing Statement clearing showing Dale as first in line on assets of the paper and its Editor, and one could, if they desired, also find a Security Agreement filed at the Rankin County Recorder's office attesting Dale's legal, financial claim.

Amos told the editor there were illegal South Americans in the community, and that as a candidate, he felt it was his duty to get the Sheriff and go out to Simmons' place and reveal the situation for what it was. Amos said he was calling because he wanted a reporter and a photographer to be there. "It is important to the community and the state," Amos said, falling back on some of the leadership and communication skills he had developed. The Editor feigned trying to get him to stand down. Then, he caved in, as if defeated.

Amos called the Sheriff. Amos knew the Sheriff knew Dale but he thought the Sheriff's oath trumped everything, and that he, the Sheriff, was like him in his quest for right over wrong, like John Wayne. But, the Sheriff and Dale had taken baths together as children, and they were both Master Masons in the same lodge.

Simmons, the son of Dale's second cousin, acted surprised when Amos, the Sheriff, the Newspaper Editor, and a photographer came out to his barn where he was working on a Smokey and The Bandit Trans Am he bought from a fellow in Tennessee. Simmons acted like he did not want them to be there. It seemed to Amos that Simmons was really scared, and then Simmons gave in to the Sheriff, and they went into the huge, high barn. There was a big, walled area in the back, right corner. It had sides and a top on it and it looked, to Amos, like it could hold fugitives. Amos heard movement, *South Americans*! he thought.

Amos walked up to the door and motioned the Editor and photographer to come up beside him with the camera and its huge flash. The Sheriff got behind them and drew his big, blued revolver. Amos yanked open the door and the photographer started shooting pictures. Amos looked back with astonishment into the Camera as the photographer captured the picture that would be on local and Jackson front pages, and the AP Wire: A perfectly composed picture of Amos, wide-eyed and flustered, and six, big, healthy Llamas behind him in the stall, clearly lit by the flash. The Sheriff put his gun away. Amos tried to get the Editor to assure him there would be no article, or picture.

The picture was on the front page the next day. The headline proclaimed, "Candidate for State Senate Cracks Down on Illegal Immigration." There was no story.

Sitting at the yellow, Formica table under the swag lamp the day the paper came out as his wife stood at the sink, feeling for him but not knowing what to do except be there for him in the moment, Amos looked down at the big picture of him and the Llamas in the background and lamented, "They didn't even have to write an article, the picture says it all. I've been a fool."

Two days later and five days before the election, allowing for enough time for the story and interviews to roll right into election day, there was a raid at Dale's chicken plant by Federal Immigration and Naturalization Service Agents. Hundreds of Mexicans were arrested, processed, and hauled away.

Local and national news crawled all over the town and area around the compound. Interestingly, the interview every news outlet wanted, was of Doug.

On CNN, Doug said, "This investigation has been going on for months but we couldn't say anything about it. Mr. Staples' council has assured me and Federal Officials that Mr. Staples' Human Resource

Department has always told him the people of Mexican origin were legitimate and legal to work in the US. Mr. Staples was perpetually shown government papers. Mr. Staples relied on his HR department, and his HR Director is the company official who signed all documents relative to Federal Regulations associated with workers. Mr. Staples signed none of those documents. The company's HR Director has been charged for Federal offenses and arrested by Federal Law Enforcement Officers. He is expected to post bond. Mr. Staples has not been charged. Many of you know I am a candidate for re-election to the Mississippi Senate, and the elections are next week. I have always said I was against illegal immigrants taking Mississippians' jobs. We are doing what we can do about this serious issue, and we will continue to do so after the elections next week."

Amos had sequestered himself since the front page picture. He was embarrassed to the core just like Dale knew he would be. Amos watched the TV in stunned disbelief. Not only had they taken his issue, they had beaten him down with it. Now that he thought about it, he was happy to be alive.

Doug won the election.

Dale drove to Jackson with his wife to take her to the beauty salon and to the mall to shop for the grandchildren. While she was having her wash and set, he drove over to James' office, without an appointment.

Sitting in front of James' desk, Dale said, "I have another DVD for you, would you like to see it?"

James responded, "Let me guess. It would be of the bird field with the little Mexican girls."

Dale said, "You are so right. By the way, the little girls were 14 years old, they tell me that's documented down there; 'tell me they know who they are."

"Where was the camera equipment?" James asked.

"In the clump of trees 100 yards to the South. You would be shocked at how powerful the technology is today. They got real close up.

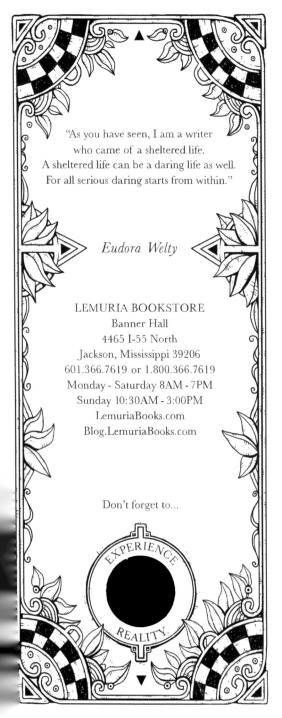

"As you have seen, I am a writer
who came of a sheltered life.
A sheltered life can be a daring life as well.
For all serious daring starts from within."

Eudora Welty

LEMURIA BOOKSTORE
Banner Hall
4465 I-55 North
Jackson, Mississippi 39206
601.366.7619 or 1.800.366.7619
Monday - Saturday 8AM - 7PM
Sunday 10:30AM - 3:00PM
LemuriaBooks.com
Blog.LemuriaBooks.com

Don't forget to...

EXPERIENCE

REALITY.

EUDORA WELTY

EXPERIENCED

REALITY.

Shocking. Did you see the clump of trees?"

"Yes, now that you mention it," James said, resolutely.

"Well, there you go," Dale said.

"You gonna give me all the recordings now this is over?" James asked, stupidly.

"Well, it is not over. This whole thing made us work a little smarter and it was actually an opportunity. We are going to run Doug for Governor next time, and then President after that because being a Southern Governor is a great stepping stone to the White House. If they can get a bumpkin like Carter, and a cracker, slim ball masquerading as a Rhodes Scholar like Bill Clinton elected, then my dumb ass, Tarzan son-in-law just might be a shoe-in. You know, James, I held fundraisers for both Carter and Clinton, had both of them in my home, broke bread with them, raised a hell of a lot of money for both of 'em. I'm gonna hold on to these films and pictures because when he runs, you are going to be my insurance policy against any shenanigans like Amos almost pulled off, and you are going to bring the state members of the Postal Workers Union to the polls for Doug, and the national members to the polls for him for President. If you need a job promotion to get the National job done, I'm sure we can arrange it when the time comes, providing you cooperate, and I'd bet you will."

"You are an evil man, Dale Staples," James said, "the worst I've ever seen. I thought I'd see a lot."

"James, you were the one in the bed, adulteratin' with two, strange women in a menage-for-three, and in the field with the 14 year olds, not I, and by the way, the child in the field with you," Dale said, pointing a boney forefinger at James' face, "they tell me he was actually a boy with long hair; you should be ashamed of yourself."
James came up out of the chair to lunge across the desk but stopped and stood there, shaking, not believing he had merged with such evil.

"Jaaaaames, calm down, you know there are copies. Don't do anything rash." Dale smiled. Dale got up.

As he got to the door, he turned on the heels of his handmade cowboy boots. "James, we goin' to the White House. You might as well settle in and get with the program."

The charges against the HR Director at Dale's plant were quietly withdrawn by the Masonic, US Attorney 6 months later. Dale paid all the court costs and the books of the court were balanced. The Masonic Magistrate accidentally let the original complaint fall into the shredder.

The plant opened back up. They gave some jobs to locals, but the Mexicans were brought back in, this time, supposedly having been vetted by the US Attorney on behalf of the US District Court.

The son of the US Attorney, a 'C' student at a private, prep school in Jackson, mysteriously got a full scholarship, including full room and board for 4 years, plus grad school, to Mississippi State.

Amos put his King's Ridge, and Hart, Shaffner, and Marx suits far to the left in his closet, and his wingtips up on the shelf. He started wearing khaki pants and dull shirts with button down collars, his collar open with no tie, and conservative blazers, only when necessary.

He stayed on at the same church for his wife's sake. He stayed on as deacon until he rotated off. He never let his name be put back in nomination again.

He started boiling peanuts and taking them to the farmers' market in town. He found he liked it because it was simple, and wholesome, and it made people happy, right then and there. They'd give him his reasonable price, happily, and it made him feel good-- his simple job, done well.

He left the picture of Barry on the dash of the last Jeep he drove on his route. It is behind the barn to this day, rusting in the weather, the picture a testament to a thing for Amos that almost was.

It is unclear if it would have been good or bad for Amos if he had won. Amos does not think about it much anymore, but he guessed one time that good or bad for him would have depended on who else got involved.

Amos was at Davis Wade Football Stadium in Starkville to watch the Mississippi State Bulldogs play the Ole Miss Rebels in the legendary Egg Bowl. He had bought himself a bag of fine peanuts and a Dr. Pepper from one of the big concession stands under the stadium and was returning to his seat when he ran right into Dale, Doug, and the US Attorney.

Amos nodded and walked on.

When Amos got to the steps to his section, he turned to see them show a pass to the police and start up the steps to the VIP Sky Boxes.

NOTE: I was listening to the radio and heard about a woman being killed in a single car accident at 2 AM in Hattiesburg, MS. It started me thinking.

"Million Dollar Burrito"

My friend Alex is a personal injury attorney. I am sitting low in a big chair in front of his desk while he talks on the phone with a prospective client. I am waiting because we have tennis court #3 at the Country Club reserved during the lunch hour. We try to play at least two times per week.

I met Alex in 1983, our first year in college. We were, and still are if you believe in it, fraternity brothers. I joined our fraternity in college to increase my odds of success in life after graduation.

Alex was in for the same reason, plus he was, and still is, a political, fraternal animal. Do not get me wrong, I liked the fraternal life and its accoutrements. But, Alex loved and devoured the life of brotherhood, especially when it came to the sisterhood, and in fraternizing with our tri-fecta of unofficial sponsors: Mr. Jim Beam of Kentucky, Mr. 'Jack' Daniels of Tennessee, and the fellow who spoke Spanish and came up to Mississippi from the Caribbean on many, many occasions, Senor Bacardi.

On the phone with prospective clients, Alex is always animated and full of bravado. His volume elevates in direct correlation with his perception of increases in expected value of a case. The tone of his voice moves toward a hybrid of 'radio talk show host,' and 'Southern Demagogue' the more he perceives a statistically significant payoff, particularly from one or more, large corporations. "I'm for the people," he likes to say when he gets revved up. He stays revved up.

Alex makes big bucks and he always needs one more dollar because he has two children in the very expensive, First Presbyterian Day School, and a wife running around in a big, lockin' differential, gas guzzlin' Range Rover. The display of stickers on her Rover's back glass is highly contrived.

The lower, left side sports her Seaside and FPDS stickers. FPDS stands for First Presbyterian Day School. The right, lower side proclaims the name, in simple white letters against a forest green background, of that camp in north Alabama to which everybody who is or wants to be somebody sends their boys every summer- Alpine, that's it.

And, oh, there is one more-- how could I forget –above the Alpine sticker. It's a white, oval, international car tag sticker with black letters --'CH' for Switzerland, because Alex took her to Basel for a conference two years ago and it changed her into thinking she is internationally distingue'. I mean, like down the blood-line of some European royalty.

Do not ask her about the CH sticker. Her lips pooch out and she will begin to talk with some conjured up accent that does not match anywhere on the planet; no, really it is not an accent, it is what my mother, who is a good judge of such things, would call a brogue. The brogue will make you want to vomit. I bring up Switzerland to her some times just for the entertainment, but never when I do not have an escape because I swear, she will go on and on with the same stories about what they did and who they met, how she emails back and forth with someone with a name like Sophi'a La'Coste, or some crap like that, and how she and Alex must go back soon for the continuation of their relationships with their wonderful, Swiss friends, blah, blah, blah.

Anyway, like I was saying, Alex always needs one more dollar because that gauche', bee-ache wife of his is always running around in the big Range Rover-- and, when I say big, I mean the SE LWB version like the damn Queen of England drives at Balmorel Castle to hunt stag, not the smaller Discovery, or the other, even smaller Rover the climbers in Atlanta drive, by toting a $700 note like a bunch of dumb asses.

Anyway, the bee-ach wife is always leaving a trail of CC receipts all over the blistered landscape behind her once, sorority-grade back-side.

He met his wife in college when we swapped with the Kappas. I remember the very night. I was there. We joked she was one of those 'with which' girls: You know the ones, they speak, 'With which this, with which that, with which, with which, with which.' She still says it when she is in what she thinks is high society, or when she's with her 'chosen and frozen,' First Pres crowd. I would like to strangle her when she gets on a 'with which' tear. She was at Ole Miss from Texas. She was a Kappa looking for Mr. Right. Mr. Right was going to need a fort of money.

So Alex is on the phone and I am waiting. I snapped out of my casual reading of USA Today about Madonna in England and how the British Press like to underscore she is middle aged, when I realized Alex is talking in his "Rush Limbaugh in front of the EIB Microphone," tone. Something big was on the line, and Alex's reel was whining so fast the ball bearings were about to melt down in the grind of the commutation.

To his business credit, Alex chummed this case on the phone to the surface by his attention to seemingly arcane details reported in the press through his knack for seeing mens rea in situations most other lawyers and everybody else miss, and by being able to identify the checkbook, or books, from where his fees will come. And, by his recognizing facts and situations that give him a higher than average probability of getting a favorable verdict from a jury of people too stupid to get out of duty. I know that's sad to say about juries, but according to Alex when he gets wound up about it, that's where the jury thing is these days.

Alex identified this case when he was casually listening to the radio and heard about the two vehicle accident that killed the young woman in Hattiesburg, Mississippi at 2:30 AM. According to the coroner's report, the woman who died was African American, divorced, 33 years old, alone in the car, obese, and wearing a moo-moo night gown, house coat, and house slippers with a picture of Michael Jackson on top of each shoe. She was an only child and survived by her mother, Ms Jones, a 15-year widow.

Alex got the deeper info by calling, then mailing a $100 bill to a young, black lawyer down in Hattiesburg who just graduated law school and sat for the Bar, and by unofficially asking the young man to find out the back story since he was in Hattiesburg and knew the black community, as he himself was black. The $100 got Alex a great return. The young lawyer even went to the funeral where he learned why the woman killed in the wreck was going out that late in her nightgown and MJ house slippers. When Alex heard about the MJ slippers, he had quipped to the young lawyer, "Crap man, was she wearing a silver glove?"

"Ms Jones," he said on the phone, winking at me, "I'm gonna put you on speaker phone so I can take notes because what you say, really, how you feel about your daughter's death, Ms Jones, is very important to me in particular, and to our firm in general."

I rolled my eyes at him. Our firm in general *is* him, and him in particular is also the firm in general, excepting his receptionist and Virginia College, Paralegal, Nadine, who loads up on margaritas at Shucker's so-called oyster bar every night after work, after having sipped 'ice picks' all afternoon at her desk like she is some Southern Belle naturally swigging sweet tea because we are in Mississippi.

Nadine once confided in me on a Saturday after we bumped into each other on the deck of the Pelican Cove Bar overlooking the Ross Barnett Reservoir, that the only time she really does not worry about drinking— worry about drinking, is the way she put it –was just before going to court with Alex, any court.

She said it was not out of respect or anything because she did not have any. It was because court is a den of snakes, and it scared the dickens out of her because she knows how corrupt the whole lot are, including the judges, she said, and her fear of this was like an anecdote to snake bite. "I could drink a gallon of Vodka on the courthouse steps and still be sober as a Baptist Missionary. It's a waste of money, plus, I have to keep an eye on all those inglorious vipers." She probably had a gallon of Vodka by the time she was telling me about the inglorious vipers. It struck me that she pronounced inglorious without slurring.

After Alex learned about the circumstances of the wreck, he sent Nadine down to Hattiesburg to visit with Ms Jones because he knew the woman to woman approach, first, would likely raise probability. The meeting being in the afternoon, Nadine took her Ice Pick in a big, McAllister's Iced Tea cup. The cup was clear. You could see the tea. It was its own camouflage.

Ms Jones bonded with Nadine as Alex thought she would, which lead to the conversation Alex was now having and I was listening in on.

Alex pressed the speaker button on the phone and put the receiver in the cradle. "There," Ms Jones, he said all syrupy like Jake Berganse. "Can you hear me well enough, Ms Jones?"

"Ya sir," I heard Ms Jones say in an unsure voice.

"Relax, Ms Jones, it's OK, you can talk to me and tell me how you really feel about this whole thing, this whole thing about your daughter getting killed just drivin' down the road to get something to eat. Ms Jones, you there?"

"Yes, I'z here."

I could hear she was softly crying, and there was a rustle on the phone that had a precise cadence. Alex heard it, too. It was unbearably annoying over the speaker phone. I mean, some things you can overlook and deal with, but this rustle really was too much. He looked at me. I rocked back and forth in my chair and pointed to the phone. He nodded.

"Ms Jones, Ma'am, I know you are upset. Are you rocking back and forth in yaw grief?"

It stopped.

"It was making a noise on the phone. I'm sorry, Ms Jones, but it was making me so I couldn't pay good enough attention to you, and I want to understand everything about what happened and how you feel about it." Alex was on the verge of gushing over board and we both knew it. But, he is a master at getting right up to the edge. He looked at me and I widened my eyes as if to say 'shut up already and move on.' He smiled.

"Ya sir," she said.

I heard the TV in her house and the beginning of the Hattiesburg, TV, Noon, News Report, and I knew there would be no tennis. I thought about leaving and finding a match at the club, but I decided to stay to hear because even though I was not sure what it was, I knew Alex smelled something big and I had learned to trust his instincts— especially when there was money involved --and being a fiction writer, I was a little curious how this episode of human drama would unfold. I was almost certain there was conflict and redemption on the way, somehow.

My itch to write fiction, the really strong itch, is only coming out of me in the several years, even though I thought about writing going way back, in and out of school. I think I have figured out the etiology of the disease: I grew up with a grandmother and mother where everything they said was connected to a Faulkneresque story you had to listen to all the way through, which could be too much sometimes, but not all bad because if you listen to people talk like that over long enough period of time, you have to write at some point or you will simply blow up when your tank gets full.

My literary tank was already three quarters full from life before coming to Alex's office. Then, this 'Lady in MJ Slippers Killed in Auto Accident in Hattiesburg' thing, had my needle moving up to full so fast I figured in the back of my mind I'd likely complete the first or second draft of another, solid short story by the end of the week.

"Ms Jones, Ma'am, where did your daughter live?"

Alex knew the answer from Nadine. But, attorneys are trained to ask questions as a method to get people talking as a manner of control by asking questions with answers so obvious, they often seem absurd.

"She lives," then she whimpered, "She lived wid me."

"Was she married?"

"Divorced."

"Children? Did she have children from the prior union?" Alex asked, with 'prior union' sounding like Matthew McConaughey, I mean spooky like MM.

"No."

"I'm sorry, Ms Jones. Just talking with you, I feel you would have been a good grandmother." This was almost cruel on Alex's part, I thought to myself, because what woman does not want to be a grandmother.

But, he was at work, I figured, throwing body blows leading to a straight, right-hand, money punch down the line and he had to build up to it. He was not after Ms Jones. He was after the morsel, or morsels, of information that make the case where they would not even have to go to court because the defendant would know a jury would surely hit them harder than almost any settlement amount.

I heard Ms Jones cry a little more audibly when Alex pushed the grandmother button.

"So, you would have liked to be a grandmother, Ms Jones?"

Damn, I thought, *dude won't lay off and move on.*

"Yessir."

"Ms Jones," Alex said in inquisitive tone. I thought, *Oh, Lord, what is this going to be?*

"Have the 'thorities informed you that the man who killed your daughter was in a company truck of a firm, I mean a company, he owned, a company that had revenues, I mean a company who brought in $16 Million last year, and that he was drunk, he was drunk when he hit your daughter's car and keeled her?"

"Naw sir, well, I know'd he was drunk after they to'ed me yes-taday, but I didn't know all dat other stuff you sade."

"Well, Ms Jones, I know this is difficult, but we must say it because it is part of the problem. That truck had a bunch of equipment in the back, so the truck was really heavy, and he was really drunk, more drunk than I've heard of in a while, and the truck was so heavy, Ms Jones, that's why your daughter's Hyundai just caved in on her fragile body and broke her so bad the funeral home man had to work on her real hard so y'all could open the casket so y'all could say good bye to her like she deserved; and, Ms Jones, I'm just reeel upset about the whole thing," Alex said as he leaned into the parting shot.

Wow, I thought, *dude putting the sorghum on thick.*

Ms Jones, probably thinking back to the wake and burial, whimpered out so we heard her.

Alex came back around the barn. "Ms Jones, I don't mean to get into this, but this whole thing really bothers me, this thing where this rich guy drinks all he wants, probably at some bar, I don't know circumstances yet, but I will be finding out so you'll know if you want, anyway, he's drinking somewhere, prob'ly throwin' hundered dolla bills around like a mobster, and then stumbles out and hits the road and keels your daughta— he might as well shot her with a gun, same thing, shot her with a gun –and then on top of all this, people got to have money to do things, even the unda'taker, and so you're the one left to bury your daughter and pay da bill, while his money buys lawyers from New York so he can try to get out of all this," Alex was on his feet talking with his hands flailing like a Pentecostal Revivalist.

He looked down at me and winked. *New York,* I thought...*Good Lord!*

Ms Jones sniffled. The sound came too loudly through the speaker and made me jump.

Alex put his head down and his hands on his waist: "Ms Jones, have you got the bill from the fun'ral home yet?"

"Naw," she said.

"Ms Jones, do you have any idea how much they charged you to bury your daughter after that rich man keeled her?"

"Naw, not chet."

"Ms Jones, they gonna send you a bill for pro'bly $10,000, $10,000 for burying your own daughter when it wasn't her fault, or your fault, she died, she was keeled. That doesn't sound fair, Ms Jones."

We couldn't see her, but at that moment in her mind, she crossed on over the river of reality to which Alex had led her, pushed by the fact she didn't have two dimes to rub together, not to mention $10,000.

Alex said, "$10,000, that's a lot, 'specially when it ain't your fault."

I heard her, "Hmph."

"Ms Jones, I'm gonna send Nadine back down there, as a matter of fact, she called earlier and she's in Hattiesburg today. So, I'm gonna send her by with a paper so we can get that fun'ral money back, so you won't be burdened by that on top of everything else. That OK with you, Ms Jones," Alex asked, having made the verbal offer and asking for her consent.

"Dang," I thought, *"'Big A' just used the $10,000 funeral costs to close contract on a settlement that will pay him no tellin' what. Da man is smooth as a glacier."*

"Yessir, I reckon, what time she comin'?"

"She'll call in just a little while. Now look, we love you up here, and *after* Nadine leaves with that paper, if you need anything, anything at all, you call, and I'll make it happen, OK?"

Mm Hmm, I thought, he ain't gonna be making anything happen without that paper.

"Yessa, OK," she said.

"Ms Jones, before I go, I am curious about something. Your daughter lived with you. You all shared household expenses like groceries, lights and water?"

"Yessa."

"Was your daughter diabetic?"

"Docta told her she was; told her right afta Christmas."

"So, she wasn't born a diabetic."

"Naw, just since Christmas."

49

"Ms Jones, where do y'all do your grocery shoppin?"

"Super Mart," she said.

"Hm, Ms Jones, do y'all use one of those Super Mart cards so you can get a discount on groceries and gas?"

"Sho, wez saves a lot of money."

"Have y'all used that for a long time, the Super Mart card that is?"

"Since they came out wid it, been usin' it right from the get-go."

I'm watching all this and thinking, *Super Mart, dude done gone crazy, what in the world?*

"Thank you, Ms Jones, Nadine'll be by to see you a little while. I'll talk with you later. I'm gonna hang up now, OK?"

"OK."

Alex hit the speaker button and the phone went dead.

"Let's go play tennis. You have time?"

"Yea, enough," I said.

Alex played above himself. He hit the ball with tons of pace. It was in court every time except two, and they only missed by an inch. A tennis clinic was on. He was the court doctor.

He served and volleyed on almost every first serve and won every one of those points by putting away clear winners, hit dead in the middle of his racket, to exactly where the highest probability shot should be placed.

When I served, he hit ground strokes so deadly and accurate he did not have to come to net. He hit winners down the line and cross court from the baseline so hotly, I could not get to them.

All this time, he said nothing, nor did he so much as grunt. His face was set confidently and placidly, with a slight smile at the corners of his mouth but he did not look arrogant. His court demeanor and play reminded me of Roger Federer.

I caught myself hitting shots to certain places on the court just to see what he would do with it, and to watch his stroke. He did not say anything when we swapped sides, nor did I say anything to him because I knew there was something bigger than this tennis match going on. I figured I would let him stay on his game in exchange for the story later, if I got it, and I figured I would, when he felt like it.

We drove back to his office where I had left my car. We got out, and the pre Fall breeze hit my damp skin with the sun mixed in. It felt good. For a fleeting moment, I thought about that girl I knew in Tennessee for 3 months an awfully long time ago, and the horseback ride we took on a fall day when the leaves were turning. I wondered where she was and what it would be like if I had married her; if I would be there; if Alex and I would have played tennis?

"I won't come in," I said, "I gotta get going."

"OK," Alex said.

I started to walk to my car. As I got out further into the parking lot, I realized I had not heard Alex open the big, squeaky front door to the office. I suddenly felt I was being watched. I turned. Alex was standing on the porch in front of the big door that would have squeaked.

I started walking back. He started down the 6 or 8 steps to the side walk. We met just in front of his car.

"You wanna tell me what is going on with you," I asked when we were 5 yards apart and closing, "You don't play tennis that well, ever."

He said, "You want to know *why* that woman died?"

I wasn't expecting him to ask that.

"I guess I do, if it's not wrong for you to say." I said.

"A burrito," he said flatly.

"A what?" I said.

"A burrito" he said.

"I thought that's what you said," then I said, slowly, "A bah-reee-toe, as in a rolled up object, available at Mexican restaurants?"

"Yep," he said.

"OK, I thought a drunk business owner in a company truck with a bunch of equipment in the back, T-boned her Hyundai and killed her," I said.

"He did," he said.

"So that's what did it, case closed, and I'm not even wondering where a burrito comes in to the mix. Oh, wait a minute, she had one, it was hot, she dropped it in her lap like that woman with the McDonald's coffee, it burned her, she swerved and he T-boned her, and he was really drunk and unlucky, to boot," I said sarcastically.

"Nope," he said, "But I *do* have that poor, drunk some-bitch dead to rights. His attorney'll call me by end of business tomorrow to get a feel of things from my side because his client doesn't have a leg to stand on and he knows it. He also knows no judge down in Hattiesburg will even think about cutting a quiet deal in exchange for anything, including, but not limited to, a grocery bag full of cash or even box-seats at the Super Bowl; it's too big and out in the open. The gal was black; there were witnesses-- a bunch of them, inside the restaurant and in the parking lot, sitting on car hoods as she was about to turn in and got busted by our drunk bastard's heavy truck."

"Look," he continued, I'm about to tell you something. It'll be public soon enough, but I'm telling you now because I need to tell someone. I'm about to piss off some really, really powerful forces. I want somebody to know about it, and I trust you— we've been friends a long time."

I was suddenly thinking, *"Do I really want to know this."*

He said, "That woman was out that morning at 2:30 or 3AM because she had to have something to eat."

"And," I said.

"Listen to me," he said, "nobody is really getting this. I am about to tell you something going on and killing people in this country, though not in conventional ways." He leaned in. "That woman was out that morning in her MJ slippers because she *had* to have something to eat."

I looked at him and said nothing.

He went on. "The big food companies are all in collusion, effectively, and they now have the technology to strike a perfect mix of salt, fat, and sugar that is driving the brains of people to have actual, hedonic experiences with the foods these massive companies put out, that then drives the people to eat more, then more, then more. It's off the hook. It used be people ate too many carbohydrates, calories, and so forth. They still do, but it is like they are super addicted and can't stop, and so 'yea, they're still getting too many calories, but now it is even more because food driven brain activities are driving them to irrationality."

"So," I said slowly, "you're saying our girl was out *so* late because she was craving *so* badly?"

"Yes, I am. I've been digging into this for over two years," he said. "I have more info on this than anyone. I know what's in what, what corp. makes what, and, I know how they process everything they put out, and how it's processed even more when it is all put together in the final, corporate, masterpiece dish, served in all these damn, corporate restaurants and grocery stores. The American food system is now the Corporate Food System. They now make food that compels people to eat more, and more. People are never sated."

"So," I said carefully,. . .

"So the girl," he said taking a deep breath, "was an obese food craver who recently went diabetic because of her life-long, food addiction that continually hits her brain just like she was on drugs; and, she couldn't sleep and got up and left her house to go get some more of her favorite fast food because her hypothalamus was going mad; and, she was so out of control she went in her gown and housecoat and MJ house shoes; and, she didn't even have a stitch of drawers on, the coroner said, and the craving, the need, put her out there where she'd never have been if she were not addicted and into the path of our drunk dude in the big, heavy truck, and he hit her so hard it ironically knocked her car into the outside tables of that damn corporate restaurant. She died within 30 feet of the trans fatty cooker making the very food that killed her."

"Whew," I said.

I didn't know what to say, so I said nothing, at first.

We stood there for a minute. I thought about how knowing him, he had it all worked out down to a fine point, and that he was probably right, even though I did not know details of what he was saying. I shook my head and pursed my lips to signal 'I heard you,' and 'it is plausible' so he would feel like he had some support, but I had a strange knowledge he did not care if he had support on this one or not, and that he was inordinately angry at an impersonal foe he didn't really know, and, that he might be mad at his foe for other reasons I did not understand. I thought how this must be a risky situation in unknown ways.

"Well, hmmm, I don't know what to say," I said. "You da pro. When you gonna pull the trigger, and how many triggers 'we talking about."

"I'll pull the trigger in a couple months. I don't know just now how many targets, but many-- it's a big monster --I'm gonna sue 'em all and let Jesus sort 'em out."

"Well," I said, "whatever I can do. Sounds like there could be black Crown Vics riding up and down your street on this one, and maybe dudes from up north looking through binoculars at you and your family at the playground and stuff like that; hec, Wilford Brimley might pull up her tomorrow in a Town Car, with an envelope full of pictures of you in compro-mizin' sitch'ations, suggesting that you should think about your few-cha." I laughed.

He smiled, "Maybe," he said.

"I'll see ya; let's play Friday."

I was walking away and almost to my car, "Hey," he said. I walked back and he met me in the parking lot. He looked around like he was in fact looking for Wilford Brimley. I felt a chill, *I think this is bigger than I realize*, I thought to myself.

"Man," he said, "my baby got diagnosed with Type II diabetes, day before yesterday."

"Savannah?"

"Yes, and she's also got high blood pressure," he said.

"She's 9," he said with tears in his eyes. "You don't have to say anything, but I know you've noticed how fat she is. I mean, when we were young, it was like the Little Rascals, you know, outa 10 kids there was 1 fat kid, now it's the other way around. She's out of control, she's addicted," he choked.

He stood there with his head hung. I did not say anything.

The cool breeze and the warm sun hit me. Again, I thought about the girl in Tennessee on the horse. I felt a little embarrassed for thinking about her at this moment of my friend's need, but to my credit, this time I was remembering what it felt like when we were young and things were simpler, and we didn't have to worry about 9 year olds being diabetic and hypertensive.

"I got info stacked up to the ceiling in there," he said nodding back toward his office. "I have some technical info about how they engineer commercial foods to hit the brain. I'm sure there's a lot more. I'll get tons in discovery after I file suits."

"Hmm" I said.

"I can't stop my daughter from eating. She'll gnaw your arm off if you get between her and those damn hedonic foods. Her mother is in denial. She chooses to believe it's a mental problem. She hit me yesterday with the news she's sending Savannah to California to some 12-step program for food addiction. She already took Savannah to a doctor we know at church because she is embarrassed and wanted to get a doctor to fix the situation. Next thing I know, they got referred around and *BAM!*-- Savannah's on an anti-depressant, high-blood pressure meds, and a 'tiny' sugar pill. Crap man, all that stuff used to be for grand mamas, not my baby."

"Hmm" I said.

He continued, "California's gonna cost $12,000 and I have to payola. It's a waste of money."

"Hmph" I said.

"Her mother is ashamed of her," he said again. "Savannah embarrasses her in front of all her Country Club and First Pres friends. That's really what this California crap is about, embarrassment. She had the damn gall the other day to tell me we had to get Savannah's weight down before we take her back with us to Switzerland. Aint' that some bs?"

"I'm gonna sue every stinking one of 'em," he said as he turned and started walking to the steps. He waved without turning around, "Thanks," I heard him call out.

As I started walking across the parking lot to my car, I heard the hinges on the big door squeak as it opened. Then I heard it slam with a new definitiveness.

The Wilford Brimley chill came over me. I was overcome with the feeling that Alex went through that big, squeaky door as if through some portal, leading to a land of new and unforeseen trouble.

NOTE: I heard something along the way in life that made me think up this story. After I had the basic idea, I needed a way to tell it, a way to tell why the narrator acted the way he did toward his wife. Barry Hannah's 'Water Liars' was the tool, the device I needed. I finished the first draft of this story while Barry was still living. I was going to show it to him. I didn't want to show him the early drafts. He was too good. I was going to visit with him the week after they honored him with the 2010, Ole Miss Conference of the book. By then, the story was good enough to talk about/workshop. He passed away the week of the event. Sometimes, my friends and I call this story, 'The Barry Hannah story.' I hope you enjoy it. Please do not let any weaknesses you see reflect badly on Barry. Put 'em on me. The characters of Marc and Sylvia were real people. I did visit them. We did go to Tarragona. Marc and I did go to the bullfights. I dedicate this particular story to the memory of Marc, my twin brother I had for a little while.

"Eight Hundred and Ninety-Nine Dollars"

When I return to Mississippi, I thought as I sat next to the window of the big jet, *I'm gonna send Mr. Barry Hannah an invoice for $899 to cover the cost of this round-trip, international flight.*

"What has Barry Hannah to do with the fact I coughed up $899 to fly across the Atlantic Ocean*?"* you ask, fairly.

"Airships" and "Water Liars," that is what he has to do with it. He wrote the stories in the "Airships" collection a long time ago, Knopf put them together, and I have a seasoned copy. As a fiction writer, I had to read it to increase my skill because BH is as a surgeon with the written word.

And, "Water Liars," the short story, is as I would have written it but a little different. But, because of that story, he is responsible for either the upcoming continuation, or dissolution of my marriage. Yep, he is the one who, through that story, made me realize I have to get out of Dodge before I do something more stupid than I already have. And he is the one who made me realize it is A-Ok to be down right sick for the love of a particular woman, while you want to strangle her at the same time. So there, invoice in the mail to Mr. Hannah for the price of the ticket because the "Water Liars" sockdolager, revealed to me only yesterday, has me on this jet, flying away to find resolution.

I saw the city coming up. We passed it and went out over the Mediterranean. I thought, "Dang, we've been high-jacked, and I don't think I'm in any condition to deal with this." Then, the big Jumbo banked hard left and the engines screamed like they were going to come off. I felt my pulse throb in my neck. I saw the huge flaps on the wings just outside and behind my window, move to turn back toward the city and the International airport which would turn out to be smaller that I expected.

The Jumbo felt as if it was sitting on its side like one of the model planes hanging by sewing thread from the ceiling in my nine year old nephew's bedroom. Being fixed above the people seated on the left side of the isle as though I was strapped into some carnival ride, I looked down at them and could see blue, Mediterranean water through their windows in front of the massive, left wing of the airship. I saw the coast line, the wharfs, the edge of the city, then the famous, Cathedral Sagrada Familia the audacious Mr. Gaudi had not finished when he departed the earth.

The pilot floated the Boeing to the runway, then drove it like we were in a big, Chevrolet Station Wagon, toward the international terminal that would be smaller than I expected. I kept thinking as we crossed runways: *I hope they got all this straight with the tower, and we don't get T-boned by some jet coming in from North Africa.*

He jerked the reins on the jet, bringing it to a quick stop. I wondered if that manner of stopping was in the training book; or, he had just thought it up on his own; or, he had to use the bathroom or something else human and ridiculous in light of the fact he was, after all, driving a giant, metal tube with big, powerful, GE engines, all weighing multiple tons and transporting hundreds of souls, including mine.

We were 300 yards away from the terminal. The sun was bright and hot, and the wind blowing like I remembered it blows in Spain. I felt the vibrations of my ancestors when the crew popped the doors like soda cans. The essence of the place rushed in, and I swore, again, that this time I was going to find those kin of mine who had come, for a little while, to the Gulf

Coast of Mississippi, USA, long ago, but hightailed it back to Catalonia and Barcelona like moths to a porch light.

We disembarked the huge bird that brought us across the Atlantic by going down ladders connected to trucks that reached up 45 degrees but felt like 90, to the doors at the front and tail of the plane. I chose to go out the back because it was different than going out the front door after domestic flights when you walk out into that tube-like hallway that pops you right up into the terminal without interface with the elements, except for the hot or cold air that squeezes though the cracks where the tube connects with the gang-plank at the plane door.

I stopped on the tarmac and looked up and under the belly, and down the length of the jet. It looked as long as an American football field. I thought about the eight hour flight over the ocean and it made me squeamish. I looked for oil leaks, or that it was dripping hydraulic fluids on the tarmac. I saw neither. I felt better about having to fly back. I wanted to walk up and pat it like a good car that took you on a trip to California and back without trouble, or like a horse you rode all day after which it looked at you out of one eye on the side of its head and hated your guts as it munched oats in the barn. But, I did not pat the plane because I did not want to look stupid, and there was nothing to pat anyway, plus we were being herded toward a shuttle by soldier-like airport personnel who looked like they would have worked for Franco, years before. I was feeling like an actor on a movie set.

I made myself last in the line to the shuttle so I could stay out in the Spanish sun on the tarmac near the under-belly of the big jet just because it was one of those situations that make you think, *When is this going to happen again?*

I arrived at the door of the shuttle and a blast of cold air from inside hit me. I looked back one more time at the looming giant. The hot sun hit my face and I smelled jet fuel. It all made me feel like an Israeli at Entebbe' in 1976. I imagined Lt. Colonel Yoni Netanyahu and his squad hunkered down in the floor board and easing up in an old, black Mercedes limo with presidential flags flying above the headlamps disguising them as Idi Amin for enough time to get the jump, and they methodically exiting the vehicle-- machine guns spitting bullets and the bullets whizzing all around --rescuing us from my imaginary enemies and escorting us away in hut-hut fashion, saving us from imminent captivity and probable death.

The shuttle had a bench seat against the wall running horizontally on each side. I took a seat, then stood, and insisted a Barcelonan senora have it for the 300 yards. She was returning home. You get to know people in a way on a plane for eight hours. I overheard her saying she had been in Atlanta, Georgia, USA, visiting relatives for a month and was returning back to her heaven: Barcelona. I thought it interesting she, from Barcelona, had relatives in Atlanta, GA, USA.

I stood in the center of the shuttle and held onto one of the straps that hung from the ceiling. I put my head down and closed my eyes and thought about how I was about to go through customs with more Franco looking officials, but this time they would have badges and guns, then navigate the airport, get to baggage claim, spot and grab my bag, then, find a taxi or shuttle into the city and to the small hotel I had reserved over the internet only yesterday, all without being able to speak any Catalan, and only a little Spanish. *No big deal,* I whispered to myself, *just get into the city and checked into the hotel and you can go for a walk on La Rambla.*

I opened my eyes with my head still down, and the first thing I saw, was a woman's sandal. Then, her foot. Her nails were painted a soft, tasteful red. It made me think of my wife.

I thought about why I was there, that I had been angry with her since before we married, and we had been married for four years. And, that the thing I have been mad about is stupid and I know it but it took hold of and consumed me in a way I am still trying to understand, and that I have never talked with anyone about it, but I think I should, and that BH's character in "Water Liars" is my kindred spirit in this stupidity, for he was, so far as I know-- since I never talked with anyone about it--my only kin, the only, other man, like me, crucified by the truth on the same tree, our tree.

My wife's foot is small, size 5 and a half. Her toes are not perfect, but they are cute and beautiful in their way. Her nails are always either clear coated or painted. She always has a biscuit-brown tan in summer, and whatever color her nails are, it happily juxtaposes against the hue of her perfect skin.

Sometimes I hold her small, left foot in my hand as I lie beside her on her right and we love. Never on her left holding her right, but on her right holding her left. I do not know why, it is just one of those routines couples fall into, and this, for me and us, is such a sweet rut.

Her foot leads to her ankle, so small and delicate, and then to a calf that is good but not of much meaning to me for some reason I do not know, but then to her thigh, oh, her thigh, I do love her thighs, though they are not very long, they are cute and mine, and we joke, lovingly, that when she is nude and lying on her side, they look like a delicious, golden, chicken thigh-leg combo, I say, and she laughs and is secure in this because she knows I am not making fun, and that I love and lust after her thighs more than any chicken, I say, and more than the thighs of any other woman on the face of the earth, including any in Barcelona, I say now.

I ride on the packed shuttle to El Prat Airport Terminal. The talk in the air sounds like the talk at the Tower of Babel must have sounded.

I am standing and I think of her toes, her ankles, her thighs, her tummy, her effervescent, white, smile, and her small, well-shaped breasts, and of them as she is getting out of the shower in Grayton Beach at the Sugar Shack last summer, and they, her breasts, looking like two delicately prepared, over-easy, poached eggs with her exquisite aureoles matching the color of her tan, and we having to shower again before dinner at the Red Bar because I had taken from the shower, onto a small bunk bed in the wall because it was closest to the bath, and we had loved, and I had held her small, left foot in my hand, this time with the toes painted a light blue like the gulf water only 100 yards from where we lay.

As the shuttle rocked from hitting a joint in the concrete on the tarmac in Spain across the world from Mississippi, I could see her that day on the bunk, vividly, as I held her small, tight bottom in my right hand and looked down upon her loving, light brown triangle. Tears welled up in my eyes and one broke free and splashed off my shoe like a raindrop hitting a moss covered rock in the deep forest, and a terror swept over me that made my throat tighten and me want to turn around and go back to Mississippi right then, but I could not, not then.

BH's character would know my terror. He said that on the morning after his 33rd birthday party during which he and his wife almost drown in Vodka cocktails, they woke up to a truth session about lovers of their respective pasts.

Being wild for his wife as he obviously was, narrator should have never, never, done that. He should *NOT* have walked into that conversation, trust me, I know, for him it was like walking in front of a Marine Sniper's nest, only 100 yards away: The bullet goes through at such velocity that it is painless at first as adrenaline is released for compensation and the victim is perversely invigorated, even while he is dead on his feet.

I sat up the first time I read "Water Liars" and the human truth in it, the truth I, too, was living, the truth I did not think a man could or would write because I thought no one knew of it. By that time, I had thought myself crazy and unable to dig out of the psychological hole into which I had buried myself.

BH's narrator said he and his wife talked about his mildly exciting and usual history, and that *he* learned she had about the same, and then he proclaimed hers surprised him because living in their era of the 70's they lived when there were supposed to be virgins in society, he was hurt to learn she had allowed anyone but him, "and so on," he said.

Then, he said the new information *dazed* and *exhilarated* him— those were his words --and he said that finally, it drove him crazy. *Amen! I say.*

He said that he was still figuring out why he couldn't handle it. *Amen, again! I say. Preach on, Oh kindred spirit!*

And then, in the high art of BH, narrator says: "My sense of the past is vivid and slow. I hear every sign and see every shadow. The movement of every limb in every passionate event occupies my mind. I have a prurience of the grand scale. It makes no sense that I should be angry about happenings before she and I ever saw each other. Yet I feel an impotent homicidal urge in the matter of her lovers. She has excused my episodes as the course of things, though she has vivid memory, too. But there is a blurred nostalgia women have that men don't."

'Tis so true, I thought the first time I read the passage, astounded someone shared my agony.

Then, from BH's narrator comes the gospel of carnal love a man has for the physical delights of his wife if and when he is raptured into her. He proclaims: "You could not believe how handsome and delicate my wife is naked."

And, then the character said he was "driven wild by the bodies that had trespassed her twelve and thirteen years ago."

Oh, dear brother, pull up a chair, I say. Let us sup together!!

But if my brother in fiction asked, I would have to divulge it was not bodies, plural, which trespassed my wife's delicate body that drove me to my wild, mad condition. It was 'body' --singular, only one.

Without my asking, for reasons having to do with the way women think I do not presume to understand, she told me, after we knew we loved each other and were committed till the end, about her loss of virginity as a freshman by a rich kid in the 11th grade; about her next lover, at college, who was younger than she, and how by her senior year, she had an apartment and he had a dorm room for appearances only because he lived with her, and that they had 'done everything,' with an emphasis on *everything.* I wondered about that but did not ask, *nor did I worry.*

In contrast, it was the knowledge of the last SOB that hit me like a sniper's bullet. I do not know why. It just did. I mean as in slooooow motion, with my heart coming out of my chest and my guts exploding with the exiting bullet, while all sounds blurred down to a crawl.

We were in a bubble of bliss until she told me of this ignominious bastard, six months before we were to marry. I was OK at first, but like it did to BH's narrator, it progressively sunk into me, and he became like a long, hat pin that kept popping the balloons of our bliss as we frantically blew them up, one by one, trying to stay ahead.

I am ashamed to say this because he was gone, I was there, she loved me, and even more strongly, she wanted me to love her. But, it is true and I cannot hide. The sniper of truth has me in his cross-hairs like I am on a wobbly bicycle and he in a bell-tower.

I hated this man. I wanted to kill him. I am still trying to understand why I could not handle it.

I wondered why she told *me*. Her telling me just before we were married was a deep thing I do not fully understand, yet I possess clues.

She offered it as if I were High Priest. She was relying on me to purify and put on the garments myself, and go into the Holy of Holies on our behalf and sprinkle the blood of the goat, drawn by lot, on the Mercy Seat to cover this thing. Then, for me to come out into the sunlight, raise my hands and proclaim, 'it is finished.'

And when that didn't work, she presented it for me to put it on the head of the scapegoat, and for me to take the goat out into the wilderness-- for us --so the thing could go away, forever, never again to roam back into her village, our village, and stick his accusatory nose of indignation under her tent flap.

But, while it seems I have some understanding of her motives now, I missed them then because I *wanted* to miss them. I ran head long into immature anger toward her and gave no mercy, exhibited no grace.

I put it on the head of the scape goat. Yes, maybe I did, but then I slung him over my shoulders and carried him around for four years and I am tired, she is tired, and we are on the verge of collapse. I am in Barcelona now and I cry out in myself, *Oh wretched man that I am, save me from my sin, for us.*

I walked the streets of Barcelona like a photographer, observing everyone and everything, not looking desperate on the outside, but gasping for redemption by watching people who were *normal, relative to me, men and women,* watching them relate to each other, begging on the inside to be free of this thing captivating my ability to live and love.

I walked for blocks. I went to the famous food market, La Boqueria. I imagined her with me as I perused the displays of beautiful and rare foods. I bought small portions of various items and ate as I walked around, she walking and eating with me, and we discussing food, la comida, as we partook, erotically, together.

I took a bus to the Montserrat, the Monastery in the mountains outside the city. I am not Catholic. Yet, I boldly walked into the Cathedral. I sat on the back pew and listened to the silence. I prayed for help almost, it seemed, to the point of sweating drops of blood.

I went back to the city and my hotel. I showered and went out in the evening and walked down to the Seashore and removed my shoes and socks and walked in the edge of the Mediterranean. The water was cooler than I expected. I felt a slight sense of hope, though hope seemed as a star, millions of miles away.

I returned to the hotel by way of various tapas bars. I ate the small foods from the sea and the land and watched the people and listened to them talk to each other. I thought of her but not of him, and I did not drink the usual four Vodka, dirty martinis, up, with shards of ice in the first pull, necessary to get the claw of him out of my mind. I did not drink at all.

I rose early the morning and took the train down the coast to the seaside village of Coma-Ruga where I had visited my German friend, Marc, and his new, German wife, Sylvia, several years earlier before cancer took him and broke my heart. I got off the train and walked the few blocks to the house in which they lived and where I stayed with them. I stood out on the small street in front of the gate in the wall looking through, wishing Marc would walk out and wave me in but I knew he would not because he was gone. I wished so badly I could talk with him because we were as brothers from different mothers, even having grown up in different countries.

I looked across the street and there were the old men in the park playing Bocce on the flat dirt. They looked the same as the day I left Marc and Sylvia. I felt like I had been gone only 15 minutes-- like I had simply walked the short distance to the small mercado for milk and eggs.

Something nudged my hand. I looked down and it was Marc's dog, the dog he and Sylvia had when I was there and that they apparently left with someone here when they had to leave quickly to go to Germany for him to be poisoned and killed by Taxol. The dog sniffed and licked my hand. He wagged his tail. He remembered me.

I sat on a bench. I put the dog in my lap. I hugged him and we watched the old men play. El perro looked at me as if he wanted to talk. I hugged him to myself and cried, long and hard and deep, as if for cleansing.

The dog and I walked down to the beach like the old friends we were. I removed my shoes and socks and we walked a long way. I remembered Marc and Sylvia on the beach with me and how they laughed and how he loved her, how she was pregnant when I was there and they did not know it, that he had cancer when I was there and they did not know it, and how they were both in the hospital after I was gone, she having their baby and he dying. And, that he did see and hold his son before he went into eternity and she had to go on living. I cried more, and deeper, like heaving emotional bile. The dog leaned into me and stayed close the whole time like a battery pulling a charge. I swear he knew. He remembered me, he did, and we remembered them.

I told my old friend goodbye and promised him I would return. I took the train back to Barcelona and to my small hotel.

I went into a sleep as deep as the universe. In a dream that played like a movie of a short trip we actually took the day before I left them to return to the states, we were at the town of Tarragona.

I did not know my mind had kept all the film intact, but it had, and I saw us as we walked under the ancient aqua-duct built by the Romans to provide water to the city. We were taking pictures and laughing in the ocher sunlight, enjoying our moveable feast of friendship and love.

We walked into town for a coffee. Sylvia told us we could go to the bullfights because she knew we loved them and she would shop and we would meet back. Marc bought the tickets at a small kiosk in the coffee shop. Marc and Sylvia hugged. She hugged me.

We trotted off to the antique coliseum like two young boys going to a county fair in small town USA. I could see him smiling widely as I remembered he did and I could see his blond hair waving in the wind that blew into Tarragona off the sea.

As I dreamed, I remembered how fortunate I had felt that day for the opportunity to go to Corrida de Toros as we had years before in Salamanca. And, I recalled we were curious how the girl Matador, Cristina Sanchez, would do and we hoped well for her as Hemingway would, even though Ernest would know the odds were against her, she in *her* dangerous summer.

Just as I remembered it, I saw that Marc and I were respectful to the citizens of Tarragona as we entered the coliseum. We said *perdona,* and *gracias* and *por favor* many times as we made our way to our seats. I again felt the extreme rushes of happiness as I sat there with my brother and we looked out to the ring and all the participants, streaming in on horses and foot, as the colors jumped out at us in three dimensions against the ancient, tan dirt. Marc had his exquisite Roloflex 35mm. He took pictures, and he let me shoot. He told me what he knew about cameras and that for me, the beginner, the Canon would be fine. He said he would mail me copies and he did. I have them to this day.

Sanchez came out and did well but Hemingway would say she needed practice but he would have respected her for the skill she did possess and for her courage because it takes courage to fight bulls, maybe even more if you are new, or not very good. Marc got close-up pictures of the action. The pictures captured Sanchez's concentration as the bull passed, close in.

Then, the dreamy film of the things I remembered ran out and everything fell quiet. Marc turned to me. He had tears in his eyes but he was smiling to assure me everything was fine: "I'm sorry you were not with us when I died because it would have been nice to have you there," he said, "I never held it against you, I know you couldn't come. Forgive yourself."

I started to cry, and as in a magic movie, people could no longer see or hear us and I knew it. So, I did not worry. I cried, for I had not known what he said until the dream. It burst me open as the rock Moses struck in the wilderness.

He asked, "How is my son? I held him right after he was born but I had to go. Do you know how he is? Does he look like me?"

"Yes," I said as I suddenly had all knowledge of his boy I had never met because I was not there the day he was born and Marc died. I had never talked to Sylvia because I did not know Marc was sick until it was too late, and he was gone, and I did not know where Sylvia was in the world and I could not afford to fly to Germany to find her.

"Yes," I said again, "He looks like you did when you were his age. He lives in Stuttgart. He goes to the same school you attended as a child. He is good in mathematics as you are, he likes cars, mainly Porsche's like you do but as I've said to you, you and he should like BMW's best," I winked and he smiled, "and right now, he wants to be an engineer, like you."

"How are my father and mother?" Marc asked.

With omniscience granted for the dream, I said, "They are old, but fine. Your father picks your son up after school and takes him to your parents' house until Sylvia leaves her work and picks him up late in the afternoon. Your father helps him with his homework. They tinker in your father's garage, and your mother brings them snacks, the same ones you liked when you were a boy. Your mother is concerned he be well rounded. So, she reads him stories late, just before Sylvia arrives."

"And, Sylvia," Marc asked with love in his eyes, "Did she find another love?"

Yes," I said, "She did, he is good to her and they love each other. They have a little girl. Your boy loves his sister, everybody is good, they are a good family," I say, feeling suddenly that our time is running out.

"When you leave," Marc said, "Tell Sylvia I love her."

"I will," I said, wondering why he could not tell her himself when we met up with her after the bull fight.

We looked out over the stadium and watched the fight. The people's mouths were moving. Many were on their feet, and the band played but everything was silent to us. We sat there watching and I appreciated the opportunity to sit there with Marc. We did not speak.

Then, he turned to me and said, "You do not know what I would give to hold and kiss and love Sylvia again. We knew something was wrong with me when you were over but we didn't know what. I went to Germany a week after you left and we found out. Those were the sweetest days after we knew what was wrong with me. We loved like there was no tomorrow because we were not sure there would be a tomorrow."

I listened. He told me the whole story I did not know. Tears streamed down my face so much my shirt collar was wet and dark.

After he finished, I could feel the arid breeze on my face coming up from the bowl of the coliseum. I could see it blowing Marc's hair. The action continued, silently. We were still invisible to the people.

He turned counselor and theologian, "The price for this thing has been paid," he said, "Why are you still charging her?"

I knew he spoke of my wife.

"Should I get you stones so you can throw them at her until she is dead?" he asked, powerfully.

I could not look at him. "Look at me," he said.

I turned. He was looking at me, his ice blue, German eyes were bright, his smile assuring, but his countenance was firm with commitment. "You go back and love and stop worrying. God will meet you there, and there will be joy."

I felt my heart lift, and I nodded my head. He smiled and put his hand on my shoulder, "I love you, my brother."

"I love you, too," I said, "I wish you did not have to go." He did not respond.
"You had enough bull fighting for today?" he asked, still smiling.

"No, not really," I said, "But I think you have to go."

We walked out onto the cobblestones. Marc stopped and turned and we hugged a big, man hug. He patted me hard on my back and I patted him hard on his. I told him I loved him. He nodded and walked away. I watched him moving through the people. He stopped down the narrow street, turned, and waved to me. He disappeared.

I turned the other way and Sylvia was standing there with their little boy who looked the spitting image of Marc.

We walked up to each other. I said, "He said tell you hello. I told him everybody was good. He said he still loves you and for me to assure you of that, but that he is happy you found love and that you are good."

She smiled at me and spoke in German. I understood every word, and I responded in kind, flawlessly. She laughed and told me I sounded like a German from Stuttgart. "I had a good teacher," I said.

I knelt down in front of the boy. I hugged him and he let me, and he hugged me back as if I were his uncle. He kissed me on the cheek. His little lips were thin and cool. His love, true.

They walked away on the same street but in the opposite direction of Marc. I watched them getting smaller. She turned around and we waved. The little boy waved, too. They disappeared around the corner.

I awoke early in the morning, full of hope, my shirt collar and pillow soaked of tears. My head was as clear as the sky over Spain.

I went to a café' and sat outside and enjoyed a cup of café' con leche' and watched the Barcelonans pass on their way to work. I was happy to be there and to see them and thought about how snappy they all dressed and how much good pride they projected. I had another café con leche' and read El Pais as much as I could but I looked at all the pictures.

Compelled since I awoke, I went to Barcelona's famous and often photographed Cathedral Sagrada Familia as if I were on a string. I felt I was being pulled up into the spires, pulled above the city.

Once inside, I took the lift as far as it went. Then, I made the climb to the tip of the tower. It was very tight at the top. I do not like heights or squeezes but I was not afraid.

I looked upon the city on one side, the Mediterranean on the other. I looked down and saw a statue of Christ. From the recesses of once closed spaces in my mind, I heard, "Behold, the Lamb of God Who Taketh Away the Sins of the World."

The wind slid though the west window like cool water. It washed across my face and body and out the east side and headed to the Sea, taking my iniquity toward my wife with it. I felt clean, and rid of the scabs that had clung to me for four years.

I stood in the wind for ten minutes, letting it cover me like the blood over the Mercy Seat. I looked out the east side. There was a rainbow over and disappearing into the Mediterranean.

I descended the spire. I reached the ground floor. I felt slightly giddy.

I said hello to everyone I saw. Surely, they thought I was crazy, an American in Barcelona, in the Sagrada Familia saying 'Hi,' 'Hello,' and 'How are you?' in colloquial, Southern US, English, as though I had just been let out of prison the day before they were to put the needle to me.

I observed another large statue of Christ. I stopped and looked upon it. Again, to my mind came words read and recorded years before: "Neither by the blood of goats and calves, but by his own blood he entered in once into the holy place, having obtained eternal redemption *for us*."

The plane landed in Jackson, Mississippi. The pilot taxied up to the tube. As I went through the door of the plane, I felt the tropical heat of

Mississippi, of home, squeezing through the cracks and I prayed because I knew I had much work to do, and that I could not do it alone.

I was at home when she came in. I had cleaned, cooked, set the table, and lit candles.

"Hi," she said.

"Hi," I said.

"Where have you been?" she asked, as if she didn't really care.

"I had to go away," I said.

"You had to go away?" she said, in agitated tone.

"I mean, I had to go away to get *me* together because it is not you, it is *me.*"

She turned her head sideways and looked at me, distrustfully.

"I want to change clothes," she said, walking away.

I poured Evian for each of us and set our plates. She returned.

I said, playfully, "Tonight's menu consists primarily of Beef Bourguignon. The chef hopes it is good, and if not, it is not the fault of Julia Child." She did not laugh or say anything, nor did she give anything away in her countenance.

I quickly continued, "The Bourguignon will be followed by a simple compilation of strawberries and real cream, conceived of and concocted by the chef and approved by the neighbor only an hour ago,"

We ate slowly. It was quiet, except she did moan a little upon her first bite of the Bourguignon. It was good.

She took another bite of Bourguignon, which told me it was really good because at that moment, she hated my guts.

"I want you to go somewhere with me," I said. Before she could respond, I slid in, "Look," I said, "let me be clear; we're on the bubble and I know it. But, we are married and have been for 4 years, and I'm asking you to trust, not to trust me, but just trust, and go somewhere I have to show you."

The big Boeing landed. Again, the plane stopped 300 yards from the terminal. She let me take her hand and I led her to the back of the plane. I stopped at the top of the stairs and and waved to an imaginary crowd as presidents do. She slapped my arm and we descended.

I told her to look at the belly of the plane but she would not do it. We boarded the tram and went through customs. Her passport had no stamps because she had never been abroad. It was all new to her. I was there with her. It was special, very special.

We took the taxi to the hotel where I stayed only a week before. We went out that night and walked up and down Les Rambles and ate tapas and drank still water and authentic café' con leche', which she loved more than I expected.

The next morning we awoke early and took the first train to Coma-Ruga. It gave me pleasure to watch her as she looked out the window to the sea and down below to the rocks, upon the occasional, small, exclusive towns along the coast far below, for she had only seen these things in picture books.

The train stopped at Coma-Ruga. We stayed seated and let the locals pass. We stepped out into the Spanish sun.

She looked to me, "Wait," I said, holding up my hand as I looked around.

Under a lone tree out in the fine, Spanish dirt, far back from the station, sat the dog. He looked at me as if to say, "I was starting to wonder." He stood up. His tail wagged. He came over.

"There's my friend," I said. She just looked at me like I was crazy.

She, the dog, and I walked through the station and down the small streets passed houses being built without insulation like we use here because it is not needed, there. We stood in front of Marc and Sylvia's house. I told her about him again. But, this time it was different.

The dog looked up at me and the dog and I missed them. We walked across the street and sat on the bench and watched the old men playing their Bocce ball and smoking black tobacco cigarettes. I could feel my unwinding from modernity.

We walked to the beach below the picturesque part of the Spanish pueblo that was hanging on and over the cliffs. We removed our shoes and walked. The dog stayed beside me, occasionally looking up at me, then to her, then back at me.

We sat in the sand at looked out toward North Africa in the spot Marc, Sylvia and I sat, years before. Her toes were painted the color of the Mediterranean. When had she painted them, I did not know.

We stayed the night in Coma-ruga in a small hotel above and so close to the sea, you could hear the waves roll methodically in all night. The dog slept on the floor at the foot of our bed.

We had magdalenas and coffee for breakfast the next morning. We walked by Marc's house again and I talked the best I could in Spanish with the man who was the unofficial owner of the dog. Then, we took the train back Barcelona, stopping at the airport to leave cargo for our return.

I took her to Montserrat and into the Cathedral. We sat on the back pew in the quiet. I prayed and I am almost certain she prayed, even through the deep lacerations of her heart. We hiked up the trail and looked back down the mountain at the monastery and I took a picture with a throw away camera that was composed so well, I had it blown up and put on a board. I have it to this day.

We got up early the next morning and went to Sagrada Familia and took the lift. We ascended to the pinnacle and looked out over the city, me looking over her shoulder since the space was tight and she, shorter. The wind came in from the west and blew over us and out the west window to the Sea. We stood in the wash for a long time.

We returned to Mississippi. I was sitting in the den of our house looking over the newspaper. The dog looked up at me as if to remind me. I stood up.

"Come on," I said.

We walked down the brick streets of Clinton to the bank and he sat outside and watched me through the glass that goes all the way to the concrete. I took care of my business and came out. "One more stop," I said.

His look said, "Yea, I know."

He went into the foyer of the post office with me because it is Ok for dogs to do so in Clinton, as long as they behave and keep a good reputation. I dropped the envelope in the out of town box. We walked home.

The dog and I were sitting in the den watching Rafael Nadal and Roger Federer battle it out on the red clay at Roland Garros. She walked in wearing a smoking, hot, sun dress, kinda short but not too. She kissed me and patted the dog on the head. He looked at me.

She walked out of the room, talking about things her friends said over lunch.

I looked at the dog and said, "That's the hot babe I love, dude." The dog looked at me, nodded his head, and one eye blinked. The dog winked at me, I kid you not. I saw it.

We named the dog Senor Coma-Ruga so we will never forget. We call him Senor. He thinks his name is cool.

I came to our bed that night. I could see her silhouette in the low light. She was nude. She whispered, "Come here."

I smiled widely the next afternoon around 2:00 PM. I figured Barry Hannah had made it to his mailbox in Oxford, Mississippi, and opened the envelope.

Tucked inside the Registered, Insured, Overnight envelope with $899 cash, was a note.

I had written: Dear Barry, Please accept this Deferred Royalty for "Water Liars:" You saved me. Thank you. Cordially, Your friend.

NOTE: Many mornings during 2010, I would go to a neighborhood coffee shop. One day as I was stirring my coffee, a splinter did, in fact, fall off my stir stick. I was looking at it when it fell. I was surprised when it sank. For some reason, I just stood there for a minute, thinking about it. The germ of this story was planted. The bank visualized in the story is right up the street. Tight, three mile area helps story work.

"Splinter"

It is Seven-thirty in the morning. I am at the local coffee shop three miles from my house, standing at the condiment island with my fresh brew.

I pour in the half and half until my medium roast is light brown. Then, I add the brown, raw sugar, not white, refined sugar, nor any fake stuff. I am 45 years old now, thinking about my health, and I believe the raw, brown sugar is better for me, relatively speaking.

I reach for the stir stick holder, go around the red, plastic ones and pull out two of the wooden ones. I put them together, side by side, to form a broader paddle. I stir. I sip.

I am about to stir again when I see a splinter on the edge of one of the sticks. It is hanging by a thread. As I watch, it falls off into my coffee.

I thought its mass had to weigh less than the surface tension of the coffee, but the splinter was deceptively heavy. It disappeared into the java abyss.

The coffee shop lets me buy a newspaper on their dime from the store next door, actually, their $.75. The deal includes me going to get it and bringing back a receipt. And, the paper stays in the shop after I leave. The house paper.

The good news for me is that I wouldn't give the paper company $3.75 a week of *my* money for their now ridiculous, anachronistic, so-called newspaper. The other good thing is I am the first to read the paper, the paper I buy with their money, and so the folds are crisp just like I like it.

As a throwback to simpler days when there weren't 1,000 TV channels and 24/7 news, and all sorts of so-called papers and periodicals, it is still a simple pleasure, though less so than in prior eras, to read the pages of a brand-new newspaper, untouched by anyone else.

I look at the front page. The usual cast are there, pushing and litigating and striving for better position on local or national or international monopoly boards by bankrupting the other side, or sides. Zero sum, economic warfare. Plain and simple.

I sip my coffee and think about how I'm getting older but that I'm not that old, and that I sometimes can't believe how quickly the world is going to pot. Not to pot like smoking pot, although that is likely true, but "to pot" as in "to the dogs," or "down the tubes."

My neck and back do not ache as much as yesterday. And, I think about what the guy said about water and salt. I swear I think he's right. *"It stands to reason,"* I think to myself because it's simple, whole and pure, assuming we're talking about raw salt, or maybe sea salt and not iodized by one of the many amoral corporations who have bastardized salt, sugar, wheat, and gosh darn everything else in the food supply, to increase shelf life and generate more profits.

I finish the paper and go back to my home-office to write up reports of my prior week's activities.

I sit in my chair a few minutes and recollect last night. I went to a home, football game at my old high school, one of the last high school stadiums in the state that still has real grass. *"$400,000 for artificial turf with a 10 year life for a high school stadium still blows my mind. The grass is part of the experience,"* I think to myself.

After the game, I waited around and went down onto the field after everyone cleared out. When my shoes hit the thick grass in the end zone, memories flooded back on me like a 10 foot wall of water. I stood there for a minute with my eyes closed. I drew in a deep breath of the scent of the grass and suddenly, I could smell the stench of my high school football uniform, my slightly minty mouthpiece, and the imbedded sweat in the pads of my helmet.

I stood there for at least a solid minute, eyes closed, while the scents took my mind back to the locker room. I saw everybody, including Wayne and Jimmy, standing in front of their lockers.

I saw the day Wayne popped Jimmy with a towel and it drew blood and Jimmy chased him down and punched him in the face and they fought in the midst of the lockers, buck naked, like two dogs in an alley until the coaches pulled them apart and they were made to run 100 yard sprints after practice until they both vomited.

We were made to stay and watch, even down to the vomiting, presumably to embarrass them, or maybe to show us what would happen if any of us did same or similar thing. But, being young, we all laughed about it and so did the coach, later, but he said not to do such things because it was hard enough to be free of injuries for a season without the risks of fist-fighting your own teammates.

I walked around on the grass and thought that not too long from then, boys would not know, as we had, how it felt to lie on their backs for per-game stretch on a thick carpet of real grass, in their own end-zone, under the lights on Friday night, when the drums beat, their hearts pounded, and the grass was perfect and thick and part of their reward for having ground it out on a hard pan practice field for months.

I took my 20 year-old Sony Walkman to the game with me. It had a cassette tape in it that had been there since senior year. During that important season, including the very last game, I used to listen to it in the locker room before we came down to the field after coach had done all the talking he could do and we were allowed to sit quietly and stew and prepare in our own way, and come to a crescendo of intensity at the moment of kick-off that we could individually and collectively maintain throughout the whole, violent struggle on the thick, perfect grass, grass that had been lovingly prepared by quiet grounds-men, spreading fertilizer and riding on mowers and kneeling down and inspecting while they thought about how soon the first Friday night would be upon them.

I put the cassette tape in. It hissed that old familiar cassette-tape hiss that would not be tolerated, today. The southern, sugary, Molly Hatchet guitars cut the silence in the stadium like a Toledo sword.

Danny Joe Brown's voice belted in my ears, "Horse kicking dust up off the trail, just getting back from a trip to Hell, six-gun she's strapped by my side, Thunder's the horse I ride, and baby, 'seems to me this is one hell of a way for man like me to earn that pay, yeah, yeah…"

My heart kicked. I breathed deeply as I stood in the center of the end zone and remembered a high kick I had received. I caught it, again, in my mind and jogged to the 10 yard line with a few zig zags, before I was taken down. I recollected my tackler and I hit the grass and that I had grunted but jumped up even before the whistle blew as adrenal hormone coursed through me like I had been stuck with an I V. Danny Joe hollered in my big, Walkman earphones, "I'm a bounty hunter, gonna hunt you down."

From tailback, I went again, made it to the 20. Then, I jogged out to the flats and caught a pass and made 10 yards before being tackled by a fast, bone crushing linebacker. I played that imaginary game down the field until I ran a dive off tackle, from the 5, for a touchdown. Danny Joe asked in my earphones, "Did you know five-hun'dered dolla's 'ill get yo head blowed off? It will, Ha-Ha-Ha." I raised my arms to signal touchdown.

Back in reality, I stood in the end zone wondering where all the time had gone? The head grounds keeper, who knew me and did not care I was out there or how long I stayed, turned off the stadium lights. I walked to my car in the dark. As I shut the door, I smiled thinking about running with the football and how 10 minutes before, I felt like I could still do it.

But, I thought about Chucky Mullins breaking his neck at Ole Miss. I shuddered. I drove away, but I thought about high school football and felt good that I still recalled, and actually felt, many of the old feelings when I was under the lights, on that thick cushion of grass.

I went to the bank just before lunch. I'm standing in line still thinking about that football field, the lights, the grass, and the smells. I'm remembering a game years before, where I was pitched the ball and deep in our own end zone,...trapped. Standing in the bank I could see the scene clearly and how big they all were coming at me, in unison, with flashing eyes and bright uniforms. My heart beat hard right there like it did that night long ago in my youth. My mouth went dry. I felt the fear and the burden on my shoulders for me to get that ball out of the end zone, and in the lobby, I could hear those three big, sweet, Molly Hatchet, southern guitars blasting "The Creeper" in my head. My history stood still. I could see the stadium. The townspeople. My teammates. They were counting on me.

Something touched me in the back of my head as I was about to step up to the teller. I turned to my right. There was a flat black, Glock semi-automatic pistol in my face.

It hit my nose. A flash of aggravation bolted through me. The big Glock was held by a man with women's stocking-hose over his head. For some stupid reason, for a nanosecond, I thought how gorgeous they, the hose, would look on my girlfriend's long, shapely legs.

My mind registered what was going on. A resolve came over me like had come over me when I was pitched the football, seconds before.

I surprised the bandit and myself. I pushed the Glock up with my right hand and came from down low with my left hook and caught the guy right in the liver. I know where the liver is and I was going for it because by then, I realized what was happening and I was afraid. This thing had to be over in a hurry. I felt his liver squish in and he squealed out similar to the sound a small pig might make. I charged him because I was terrified I was going to be shot.

We joined and started going back. We went through two velvet ropes. People screamed and scattered. The marble table from where you get deposit slips and fill them out, was coming up, *FAST.*

He was falling and I was churning my legs like the tailback I was, as if we were on the three-yard line and it was all down to this. As I drove us backwards, my mind wondered, as the human mind often does in such situations, what the devil I was gonna do when we stopped, wherever we stopped.

The bank robber was quiet the whole time.

He rammed into the island with the back of his head.

His neck broke, probably like Chucky Mullin's, but more drastically, because it was total and clean. I heard it. I felt it.

The tearing of his sinewy materials felt and sounded to me, like when I pull the big turkey leg off the bird at Thanksgiving by twisting and ripping the connective tissues surrounding and holding the joint. The breaking of his neck made his head unnaturally release back toward me, opposite our mutual momentum, and his body accelerated even faster against the table until his chin was on his chest and it could go no further.

He fell straight to the floor like a 50 pound bag of rice.

His grip went the instant he died. The black gun flew into the air, came down, and hit the floor, sounding like a toy against the marble floor of the finely appointed bank. Out of the corner of my eye, I saw it slide, like a hockey puck, all the way to the back wall.

I hit the island with my chest but bounced off and sprawled out in the floor, right in front of the table. The guy was dead, instantly. He looked like a rag doll, yet with panty hose over his head.

I felt sick. I knew I was going to vomit. I jumped up, ran outside and threw up, violently, right outside the door, all over the expensive shoes of a woman who was reaching for the door to come in and make the deposits from her dress shop business in the strip center next door.

I see her all the time and we speak. But, I could not talk, for I had just killed a man, thrown up on her shoes, and my vomit had splattered her chins.

I ran to my car and drove away. I remember thinking that leaving was not the thing to do, that I had just killed a man, but I remembering rationalizing that everybody in the bank knew me and they saw it all and there were, undoubtedly, cameras and they would reveal it was self-defense. The police would come to my house if they wanted to talk because the bank would give my address, etc.; it sounds crazy, but that is what I thought. I wanted to be in my house, my home, as though I had been out of town, far away, for a long time.

I arrived and my neighbor was washing his fishing boat. He drinks red wine all the time for his heart, he says. I don't even drink. But, I went straight in and got a big Ole Miss stadium cup and walked over to him and held the cup out like a beggar for alms. "May I have a full cup of your red wine?" I asked.

He looked at me, quizzically, "Sure, why not?"

He took the cup and before he disappeared into his house, I said, too loudly for my own tastes, "Can you please fill it to the brim?"

I remember all this now. I didn't really know what I was doing. I mean, I was looking a gift, wine-horse in the mouth. I do not usually do that type thing. I'm appreciative. But, I had just killed a man. I had never done that before. This was new territory.

He brought the cup back and I said 'Thank you.' I turned around and walked back to my house and sat on my front porch. He started washing his boat again but he kept looking at me out of the corner of his eye. I don't blame him. I'm just saying that's what he did.

Sure as Austin City Limits, I heard the sirens coming. The police barreled up in front of my house, two cruisers, angled in behind my car in the drive way to block me in. *Like I can really drive*, I remember thinking.

My neighbor was wide-eyed as Rodney Dangerfield when the Five-O actually stopped in front of my house. He stayed out there waving his rag over that boat in one spot, like he was washing it, just so he could hear what was going on and see the action. You can't blame him. It looked ominous, really, like I had Machine Gun Kelly holed up in my house or something like that.

Nosy neighbor had the chance to rubberneck without actually rubbernecking, so he took it. Can't hold that against him. I'd likely done the same thing if the shoe were on my foot.

I was steadily sipping that wine. Looking back, the adrenaline was dying down and I was starting to shake like a leaf. I'm surprised I didn't loose my bowels. I mean, I just killed a man who had a stocking over this dang head. Like the stocking makes any difference. And, I had felt and heard his neck break and it was the momentum I created, plus our combined body weights, that severed his spine.

Speed times mass equals force.

I didn't move when the cops got out of their cars. They were young, with military styled haircuts like many cops wear now, but never did in the past, because military and police are very different. People have forgotten this. But, it is still not right, like artificial turf on a high school football field is not right.

They looked at each other as they made their way up my driveway. They knew me, but not well. I knew them, but not well. It's a small town.

They had their holsters unsnapped. I noticed. It made me take a another fairly large drink of the wine. Actually, I pulled on it like a like a fat, Southern Baptist drinking sweet, iced tea at a summer dinner-on-the-ground.

Po-Po number one calls my name and says to me, "Sir, you all right?"

"No," I said, "Why do you ask?"

"Sir," Po-Po number 1 says, "Can we ask you some questions?"

"Go look at the surveillance tape," I say, "I'm sittin' right here, I just realized I can't walk, I can't feel my legs."

"But sir," Po-Po 2 said, "We have to ask you some questions."

"No, you do not," I say, "You know what happened, there were cameras everywhere, witnesses galore; my gosh, why do you want or need to talk with me? I feel sick and I can hardly talk and I don't want to. I couldn't add anything to the film worth knowing, anyway."

Po-Po 1 and Po-Po 2 looked at each other and shrugged their shoulders. I kid you not, they walked away, got in their cruisers, and drove off.

I remember, I looked over at my neighbor and he was standing there with the water hose in one hand, the sponge in the other. The water was squirting up in the air like on a TV commercial. His jaw was dropped like he'd seen George Washington ride up on a horse.

I just sat in the rocker. I couldn't move.

I sat there like the Lincoln Memorial, I mean I was washed out. Hec, I had just killed a man with panty hose over his head-- like the panty hose make it any better or worse --but you gotta admit, the panty hose add a touch of something to it, maybe irony, I don't know. But, I had just killed him, and I heard and felt his dang neck break, and the other weird thing was, the dude didn't budge. I mean deader than dead.

It was like he was a robot and I cut his red wire: Bam, shut down. I thought about that later. I'm not kidding. I mean, *cut, his, red, wire.*

Back to the neighbor. He never said a word. I didn't either.

When I finally went inside, I stupidly thought I would revert to normal life and do whatever it was I would usually do, but I was sadly mistaken. I walked directly to my bed and collapsed with my Ralph Lauren, blue blazer with gold buttons still on. I immediately fell into a deep, deep sleep. I mean a Black Hole sleep, like when you slobber all over the pillow. I slobbered all over my pillow.

I woke up and it was late in the afternoon. I was starving.

I went to the grocery store, still wearing my Ralph Lauren, blue blazer with gold buttons.

Everything looked comical. I just killed a man, heard and felt his neck break like 35 sprigs of angel hair pasta held together in your fists and broken before you drop them in the boiling water, and I'm at the dang grocery store, ridiculous Muzak playing in the background.

I was feeling like quitting my job and going to the airport and flying off somewhere to run a beach umbrella, rental operation someone else owned, for cash. 'wear espadrilles all the time, zinc oxide on my nose, and Ray Ban Aviators like we use to. Take the proceeds from the sale of my car and buy myself a simple, townie bicycle with a basket on the front for my possessions-- ride it around when I wasn't manning the beach umbrella stand. I'm being serious; I was already trying to remember where I stashed my passport.

I walked around the corner of isle 13 and ran directly into my ex-wife and a precious, little girl about 6 years old. I had not seen my ex wife in 13 years, since the day we shook hands and nodded to each other like a couple of damn, Japanese businessmen at my lawyer's office after signing the papers, dissolving the contract.

She would have preferred not to bump into me. I could have done without bumping into her. It was too late.

"Hi," I said.

"Hi," she said back as she looked uneasy and hugged the girl to her legs.

I looked at the little girl. She was looking up at me. She said, "Hi."

I knelt in front of the little girl. My mind realized she was my ex's child I heard through the grape-vine she had with her new, perfect husband, except he was not perfect and she did not know. Or, maybe she did?

We had no children together, nary a one.

"She your baby?" I asked my ex as I looked up at her.

"Yes," she said flatly.

"What is your name?" I asked the little girl. She told me.

I told her mine, my first name. Then, I said, precisely without contraction, "It is nice to meet you." She stared at me with big, sky-blue eyes, eyes like her mother's.

Having just been confronted with crime, death, aging and nostalgia-- all mixed together in a big, black, immoral, existential witch-pot --I was suddenly mesmerized by the delicacy and perfection of her skin and hair; her little white teeth; her perfect hands; and, it hit me like a sledge hammer, that this little girl could have been my little girl.

It was on the razor edge of what I could bear at that moment in the public, in the dog gone grocery store, that was already absurd to me because although in self defense, I had just killed a man with panty hose still over his head, when his neck snapped at the location his neck connects to the rest of his spine just inside the back of his shirt collar, like a bamboo shish kebab stick you can buy on isles 13, and I never got a look at his face, nor did I know his name.

He never said a word to me. Nor I to him. He died. I lived.

The little girl, who could have been mine, did not know all this, nor could she, I knew, but I was convicted by her stare. I wanted to run away from her innocence because it made me feel like Adam and Eve must have felt in the Garden, when God came looking for them after they had eaten the poisoned fruit.

I regretted feeling so unclean at that moment because I knew I would never see her again and I wanted to talk with her and see what she was like so I could have a moment, a second, to feel she were mine, although she did not have my genes, but the genes of another man. But, she was from her mother, and I knew a little about that because we were married for 6 years, before the wolf came to our door.

I could feel the tears coming like a storm creeping over the prairie. I stood up and said, "Excuse me."

I walked away immediately. I did not want my ex to see me cry because I had heard and could now see, that she had a smug air about herself because she was remarried, had two children, and hubby's family has money. I did not want to talk about myself and chance being compared because I was still a divorced bachelor, living in a small place, somewhat like a hermit, working, and licking all the paper cuts I had collected over the years.

I went to bed and slept all night. I dreamed a dream like a movie reel of my whole life. I have no idea how that happened because it had never happened before, but it did.

I awoke the next morning and took a walk. I came back in and sat at my desk. The half-full, Styrofoam coffee cup from the previous day, the day I killed the man with the panty hose over his head whose name I did not know, was still there beside my computer.

Not having made coffee or gone to the shop, I poured the coffee into a mug and microwaved it.

I sipped it. It was good, good enough.

Thirty minutes later as I took the last drink from the mug, there was something on my tongue. I used the tip of my index finder to retrieve it.

I looked at my finger. There, was the splinter that had fallen into my coffee the previous day, the day I had killed the man with the panty hose over his head, the day I had seen the little girl who should have been mine.

I had forgotten about the splinter.

The splinter was very small. I put it on the edge of my laptop.

It stood out against the black skin of the computer. I looked at it and thought about the little girl, and how things we think are gone, come back on us.

NOTE: I continue to be fascinated by the fact that in order to experience intrigue, physical and psychological risks, and dangerous, human action, we do not have to go to Central Europe, pack a Walther PPK, and tear through the streets in a BMW M5. All we have to do is look next door; or, down the street; or, in our own living room. Love, greed, fear of loss, and other, complex, human emotions are potent. Hitchcock sits on on a bench in the town square, waiting. I know a couple who have a fence and a neighbor. The wife made a comment one day. Just a comment. It got me thinking.

"The Tall Wooden Fence"

Nic is 46. He was married once, years ago. "Things happened," he says, if asked.

They had no children. Afterwards, he lived alone for years. Sometimes he felt old from the whole thing.

One time he was chemically depressed for months and did not know it until a friend in the medical business pointed out that he exhibited tell-tale symptoms. "I do?" Nic had asked.

He never saw himself as someone who needed a shrink. But, the next thing he knew, he was in the waiting room, filling out forms. He was surprised and intrigued that one of the questions was if he ever thought about suicide. He looked at that question for nine minutes. He read the other questions. He realized he *was* depressed, but according to the form, not to the point of jumping off a building.

The doctor sat behind his desk. He wore street clothes. No white coat. No couch. No questions about how Nic grew up, or if he hated his parents. The doctor's mode surprised Nic. He had not expected it.

The doctor told Nic he did suffer depression but not too badly and that only 10 mg a day, for about 3 months, should put the wind back in his sails. Nic managed a slight smile.

He thought the sail analogy was accurate. He had been feeling as a once grand, now dilapidated, wooden, sailing yawl, sitting motionless in the nautical center of the saline, Dead Sea, baking in the Middle Eastern sun. Sextant rusted. No radio.

The doctor gave Nic sample meds from a closet and patted him on the back as he walked him to the checkout counter.

The next day, Nic had to go to his father's house in the countryside to feed his dog because his father was out of town. Nic saw the bluish-black, .357 revolver, with its ivory grip, in the drawer, the drawer his father kept the key to the utility building where he stored the dog food. Nic suddenly thought about how better things would be for everyone if he were not around.

He actually tried to decide temple?, or mouth?, and it terrified him. He ran out the back door and kept running through his father's pecan orchard. He ran for 20 acres, finally stopping only because he came to the very back fence where the property ended and was bordered by a wide, deep, impassable creek. He stood there, crying and breathing heavily like a horse that had outrun a lightning storm across a giant, western plain.

After some months, how long Nic doesn't remember because he is not one to catalog such things, the fog lifted. He started to notice, again, how pretty the sky can be; how delicate, flawless, and beautiful the skin of a 4 year old is; how many different colors a flower can really have, and how bracing and fortifying a cool breeze felt on his face.

He met her after his fog had lifted. So, he was capable of seeing her beauty. The first, physical thing he noticed was her flawless skin, *how could that be?,* he had wondered; and, *her lips*, he would think, *how utterly perfect,* he had silently observed.

He would steal looks at her. He wondered how she, being so gorgeous, could be single at their age. He learned how the other man-- there had been a husband --had been self-absorbed and unaware of her value, and that he had violated her trust, probably many times but Nic did not care to know the full story. He felt too old to worry. So, he didn't.

Nic and she married. She had the better house at the entrance to a middle-American subdivision. Her house was decorated as she liked. Nic sold his house.

It was spring of the year.

Everyone adjusted to their new life together, including her cat, which would leave her usual spot at the foot of the bed at bedtime for a place on the top of the dresser where she would watch, with disgusted countenance, the new couple in their, big, four poster bed, high off the floor like the bride liked it.

Nic would almost always arrive home first in the afternoon. When he did, he would open the dining room blinds so he could look out over the back yard as he cooked dinner for them, for her.

He liked it when he heard her car door close. He would watch her through the window. It agitated him that she liked to get the mail first because he wanted her to come inside. He smiled as she would stop to look at her flowers. His heart would rise as she walked past the window and pretended she did not know he was looking at her, all over-- hungry like the wolf --even though she knew he was because he had told her so one night as they nestled together on cool sheets, bathed in moonlight that streamed through their window.

He would listen for her to come in. She would open the door and his pulse would quicken. He would hear her say, "Hello Kitty." She'd set her keys on the antique hall tree he bought for her.

He had laughed a few weeks earlier when she admitted she did not know how to send or receive text from her smart phone and that she had asked a younger colleague at work to teach her. Nic forgot their conversation about texting.

Two days after her admission, he laughed out loud on a highway outside Oxford, Mississippi as he pushed his 535i to get home to her by 5:30, when he read her very first text to him: "Yo dog, what's up? You hungry? I'm starving?"

Nic had texted back, "Hungry for you."

She managed, with fingers unfamiliar with the keyboard, "I'm glad."

She loved and collected beautiful dishes. Nic had none, but he had traveled many parts of the world and cooked in those places and he loved to take great care with her China and set a pretty table for them, for her, by the window in the spring afternoons after work. They would eat slowly, and talk, and listen to music, and sometimes they would go for a walk, sometimes not.

After dinner, he would shush her to the den in an old fashioned sort of way. They both liked it. She would relax and play with the cat. He would put the dishes in the washer and tidy the kitchen as he listened to the news on the radio, or to music on the occasions he was fed up with commerce and politicians.

A playful ritual developed between them. Later in the evening before she was too sleepy, she would disappear into the house and he would go find her. When he did, he would hold out his hand and she would take it. They would go to her bath room and he would start her water, warm but not too hot, and while he made the water perfect, she would stand in front of the big mirror and begin to undress.

When she got to it, he would stand behind her and unhook her bra. She would cross her arms and it would crumple and she would shrug her shoulders in and it would fall and she would catch it and fold it neatly, one cup on the other, and put it on the counter. He would look at her in the mirror and she would let him. It made her happy and warm all over that he desired her.

Nic would undo her hair. She would gently shake her head. Her hair would release and fall. He would say, in a whisper as he ran his fingers through it as if they were a comb, 'capelli bello.'

From behind her, he would slip her stylish panties down just past her bottom. She would turn one hip, slightly. Then, elegantly flex one knee toward the other. Her panties would fall to her ankles. She would step out of them in a haute' couture way.

He would slide his hands up and down the outsides of her hips, looking down at them as though he had discovered a treasure.

She would lift her arms up and over her shoulders and around his neck so that her hour-glass figure was on display in front of them, in the big mirror. He would caress her bottom and tell her he loved her. Then, he would put his arms around her waist and softly tickle her tummy and breasts as he kissed her shoulders and looked into her eyes, eyes no longer her own, but of the mythological nymph she had become, beautifully displayed in the mirror.

She would pick up her fallen hair and give him her neck, her eyes saying without sound, kiss me, kiss me. He would and she would moan, slightly, saving the balance for the night.

He would pull her close as he kept watch over her in the mirror. She would turn her mouth to his and they would kiss deeply. She would giggle, then look come-hither-ly, again, at him in the mirror.

She would coo like a happy cat as she stood there for a moment, naked except for her hair.

He would release her. Her water ready, she would gracefully step into her tub. He would watch her, thinking every time of a masterful, European oil on canvas he had seen in the Louvre in Paris, years before he ever knew her.   He had stood in front of and admired it for some time.

She would lean back into the warm water and moan with pleasure. He would stop at the door and look at her and smile and leave her to her bath and go into the other rooms of the house. He would smile as he listened to the soft humming of her angelic, soprano voice as it wafted through the air of their house like the fragrance of spring flowers.

These were, as Nic had said to her, their halcyon days of love.

Their ritual continued after her bath. He would be in the den reading, or at the kitchen table with his laptop, and she would come in from her bath, her hair damp and in a fashionable clip, and her body clean and naked in a thin, summer robe, barefooted with her toes painted a pretty color to match her fingers, and he would always wonder, at that moment, why he had been alone for so many years. She would have the sash of the robe tied tightly around her waist. He could see the hour-glass curve of her body and her breast, pushing against the fabric, her cleavage always peaking out at the top.

He would shower and put on a small amount of cologne she bought him and he would follow her to the bedroom. She would stand beside the big bed and drop her robe. The cat would watch them from the dresser.

He would rise first in the morning and prepare breakfast and set the table by the window with her china, more simply than for dinner, and she would come in and they would eat quietly. Then, she would put her hair up and they would shower together and he would lather her voluptuous body that he had come to crave, rubbing her all over with fragrant soap; sometimes, they had to shower twice.

This sweet routine of their life carried on in the spring and as the summer approached, he noticed in the evening after he heard her car door shut, that she would, as usual, get the mail, inspect the flowers, then stop and gaze toward the north side of their house.

He was on an extension ladder leaned against the house cleaning the gutters the first Saturday after he noticed her gazing to the north. From the top of the ladder, his gaze was naturally drawn over the tall, wooden fence separating their yard from the neighbor's. He could see the neighbor's backyard. He could see it very well.

During the beginning of spring while he and his new wife were engrossed in their new, amorous life, the neighbor had built a pool. *I didn't realize that*, he thought to himself.

The pool was concrete, not too large, and kidney-shaped. *High style,* he thought, thinking Barry Hannah might have described it that way. He hated he could no longer drive up to Oxford and meet Barry at Square Books and go up stairs with him for a coffee and listen to Barry's pithy comments and marvel at how adroitly he handled every question from any and every who always gathered when Barry was out and about.

The bottom of the pool was painted a deep, royal blue, and it made the water look delicious, as though you could drink it. *That's nice,* he thought. The lawn was landscaped all around. There were rocks from out west, and cacti and furniture, and though it was daytime and they were not lit, the whole design and construction was made complete by architecturally placed, ground lighting. He could see the small fixtures peaking out from the rocks. "Slick," he whispered into the cool air.

She came out the back door onto their deck and looked up at him on the ladder. "What are you looking at over there?" she asked.

He climbed down. "Climb up and have a look; I'll hold the ladder."

"What is it?" she asked.

"You'll see."

From the top of the ladder, she looked into the neighbor's yard. She looked down at Nic. Then, she leaned her back against the ladder and folded her arms as though she forgot she was eight feet off the ground. She gazed into the yard, taking it all in for a long time.

"When did they do that?" she asked.

"I don't know. A crew would have done it during the day, when we are gone."

"Darn," she said, "I like that."

"It is pretty," he said. "I like the color of the pool. It makes the water look inviting. Inviting, that's a good word for it," he said, as he made a mental note to use the word in his current story, when it fit.

"That's why they've been hanging towels and other things on the fence," she said. Then she blurted, "Darn, Nic, their yard looks like a magazine."

"They did do a good job," he said.

Still on the ladder with her arms folded, she said-- as she had the first time when a storm had come and a limb damaged the fence --that she and her first husband, she said his name from atop the ladder and Nic winced, had the fence built years ago, and that she had worked overtime to help pay for it. After she said it and still leaning back with her arms folded, she continued to look over the tall, wooden fence into the neighbor's back yard, and the blue abyss of the new pool.

"We had a hot-tub one time," she said.

Nic felt the back of his neck tighten when she said her first husband's name, again, and that they had the fence built, and that they had a hot tub. "*Great, hot tube,*" he thought, as visions of lamp light, sounds of music, and grainy images of her nude, wet figure, writhing in the water played in his mind, accompanied by her erotic giggle, his giggle, then, in *their* new, erotic life of love and happiness.

He took one hand off the ladder and rubbed the back of his neck like an actor in a tension-headache, TV commercial.

He made breakfast the next morning. They went to church. They held hands like teenagers. She would squeeze his hand when she heard something she liked. He would smile and squeeze back.

They went to brunch. Then, to the independent bookstore where they sipped coffee in their own little corner. Nic quietly read passages to her from Larry Brown novels, Barry Hannah and Ray Carver short stories, and from Hemingway's book about his Paris days.

As it always did, reading fiction aloud made Nic excited for it as if for the first time. "Yes," Nic said to her in low voice but not so low as a library voice, "Brown is gritty; he's lit, but he's gritty for sure because he writes about common people like Faulkner did, but the times their characters lived are different; Barry slashes when he writes like a great running back. I think he is greater than most people realize. People should read him more. Barry told me that reading Hemingway can teach you economy- Barry told me that because I needed it at the time; and Carver, well, Barry said he re-energized the short story and made it acceptable again- Barry told me to read Carver, too, because he is economical like

Ernest but not exactly the same way, and Barry said I could learn the short story by reading Carver. I wish I could have told Barry 'Thank you' again for that advice, but he passed away and I missed my opportunity."

They read from books they loved as children and more recently, as adults. He told her he would not read to her again until she read to him, and she did, in an intimate nook at the very back with them surrounded by tall shelves to the ceiling, full of books.

They each bought a book. When they were in the car before he backed out of the parking space, he handed her another, neatly gift-wrapped by the store's staff while she was not looking.

"I think you'll like this," he said.

She slid her nail under the tape at each end and taking great care, she slid the book out as a young girl wanting to keep the paper for her hope chest. She looked at the hard, permanent cover, then at him.

"It's the Hemingway in Paris book, the one I read from that you liked" he said. "I hope you like it all. It is the book that Hemingway tells of the interesting times and people in literature when he was starting to write fiction. He was married to his first wife when he wrote it. He tells of Gertrude Stein, Scott Fitzgerald, and others."

"Will you read it to me?" she asked.

"If you want," he said.

"I want," she said.

"When?" he asked.

"Tonight," she said.

"When tonight?" he asked.

"While I'm in the bath," she said. "You read to me about Paris while I am taking my bath."

"Ooooo," he said as he slowly backed the car. He thought of the painting.

They let the top down and put in 80's music they grew up to and took a ride north, up the Natchez Trace, almost to Kosciusko, occasionally stopping along the way at the rest areas where, if no one else was there, they would put the top up, leave the car, and walk on the boardwalks into the woods. They would flirt, make out, and casually read some of the US Government made signs telling of the place and its historical significance.

At the third rest stop on the board walk above the water in an ancient cypress swamp full of Indian spirits, they were making out and he put his hands under her skirt and down the back of her panties and held, rubbed, and kneaded her bottom as they kissed, deeply. After a few moments, she giggled and pulled away and started walking back toward the car. She turned and looked at him. Her eyes looked slightly wild.

She started to run away, up the boardwalk. He followed but he did not get too close. Near the end before the boardwalk broke out into the open to the parking lot, she stopped and looked back at him, her eyes more wild than before.

She reached under her skirt. With one, smooth motion, she pulled her panties down, stepped out of them, and waived them, tauntingly, at him. She left them on the handrail as she turned and continued her jog to the car.

He came to her panties and scooped them up and pushed them down in his back pocket. When she got close to the car, she heard the doors unlock as he pressed the remote from down the hill. She opened the door. She turned around and sat down on the seat and her skirt was up and he could see her nakedness from where he was, and when he got to her, he could see her veins and arteries pulsing in her neck.

She looked up at him and he down at her. He looked around and there was no one else.

He reached down and ran the electric seat back as far as it would go and reclined the seat back all the way horizontal. She watched him do it as he was preparing it for her. She tugged at his shirt, whimpering slightly, her eyes red. Her eyes hot. She fell back into the reclined seat, her left leg over the console, into the driver's side of the car.

He got in and knelt on the floorboard in front of her. Her skirt was up. She pulled the front of her blouse down and took her breasts out. They glistened with perspiration. She held one in each hand and looked at him like a vampire, her eyes wild. Her eyes red.

He dove into her with desire as primal as the wild Indian, as vicious as the marauding highwaymen who had been there, at that very place on the Natchez Trace, 175 years earlier.

They arrived home late in the afternoon. It was still light. They parked in the driveway as they did everyday because the garage was full of antiques she had collected before they married and they had not figured out what to do with them. In coming and going, they would walk around the side of their house on stepping stones to the back door off the deck. The deck overlooked the back yard.

They were holding hands as they rounded the corner. He was looking at her and she was looking ahead and as they came to the short steps to the deck. She dropped his hand and stopped in her tracks like a horse encountering a snake.

He followed her gaze to the tall, wooden fence. Hanging over it were three, very large, garishly colored beach towels, and a big skimming net with a bright, aqua-blue frame, conspicuous against the wooden fence.

He looked back at her. Her face was flushed.

"I wish they would quit hanging towels and things on my fence. It's ugly," she said. "We built and paid for that fence. He's just using it."

Nic felt his heart sink.

She stomped onto the deck and disappeared into the house.

Nic stood there, looking at the gosh-awfully colored towels, and the net. Bud Light and Carlos' and Charlie's logos blared back at him from the towels. *"Poor Natalee Holloway,"* he thought to himself.

He took a green, five gallon pickle bucket from under the deck and walked over to the fence. He could hear talking, shouting, and big splashes as revelers jumped off the diving board.

Nic stood there for a moment trying to decide if that moment was a good time to say something. Or, if he should let it pass and go over later, more formally, and ask the neighbor to remove the things from the fence, and to refrain from putting anything on it the future.

He had met the neighbor and talked with him one day for 15 minutes as both happened to be in their contiguous, front yards. To talk had seemed a natural thing to do.

Nic remembered that the neighbor was nice enough, and that they were about the same age but had graduated different high schools in different, smaller towns on opposite sides of their larger, metropolitan area. Nic recalled that neighbor and his wife had two children: One girl in high school, and one boy attending a local junior college, studying criminal justice while working as a local policeman for their small town of 25,000.

Nic remembered the police boy. Nic thought he looked like a child. It seemed strange the boy carried a Glock. 45-- he looked so young. *And, he has a squad car,* Ni thought, *parked next door because he lives with his parents.*

Nic looked through one of the spaces in the boards of the fence and saw his neighbor sitting at a table under an umbrella. Police boy was on the diving board. David Lee Roth era Van Halen played from a boom box on a picnic table near the back door.

While he pulled back from the crack in the fence and thought what to do, the Van Halen of his youth made Nic's thoughts digress. He remembered seeing a live, Van Halen show in 1983 and that he got back stage with a friend whose father was local FBI and could get them in anywhere, and that he had met David Lee Roth and how much bigger than life Roth seemed close up, as he swaggered around with his fifth of Jack Daniels. *Police boy was not even born then,* Nic thought.

Nic left the green, five gallon pickle bucket by the fence. As he opened the back door to go inside, David Lee proclaimed, "I live my life like there's no tomorrow."

Faintly, Nic thought he smelled Jack Daniels. He closed the door.

It was dark and cool inside. She was not in the den. He heard her in the kitchen. He looked in. She was pacing the floor with the cat in one arm, her cell phone in her other hand, talking to her sister who lived three miles away and knew everyone in town, including their neighbor.

"They hang towels and nets and stuff on my fence all the time," she said to her sister. Nic tensed.

Sure enough, she said it: "I worked over-time and *we* paid for that fence, and..."

Nic turned and made for his study to write the ending of his latest short story that had been brewing in his mind all day.

Around nine, he went to the guest bathroom. He saw she had showered there the day before and that as was sometimes her way, she had stepped out of her jeans and panties and left them right there in the floor as they came off her milky body, the lace panties still in the jeans. He observed one leg of the jeans stretched out, long, and he thought of her legs.

One of her $200 bras was there, too, on the floor as it had fallen from her breasts and off her body and landed beside the panties, still in her jeans. The bra was lacy. Sea foam in color. He recognized it. He had unhooked it. He picked it up and rubbed the lace between his thumb and index finger, then, on his cheek.

He observed new, pink flip flops, neatly stepped out of. They made him think of her shapely ankles and pretty feet. He thought of her, nude and bending to turn the water on, of her regulating and checking the temp, touching the water, probably with her right hand as she pulled and held the curtain back with her left as her breasts hung, pendulously.

He peeked behind the curtain and saw her favorite shampoo. He leaned in and picked up the bottle and smelled it. He thought of her delicately stepping in as a doe in the forest, her naked body under the water, and her scent after a shower. He looked at his watch. He forgot his short story.

He went to her bathroom, their bathroom, where he runs her bath and holds her in the mirror and where she steps into the bath as though she is a happy, European nude.

He turned on the water and he could *feel* her stir in another room and shortly, she came in, but with a furrow in her brow; nevertheless, she came. She took off her clothes, and setting aside some of their ritual, she stepped into the tub and he pulled up a chair and took the book about Hemingway in Paris and began to read. Out of the corners of his eyes, he could see her beautifully shaped breasts, the curve of the sides of her waist giving way to the wider and perfect shape of her hips, and her dark blonde triangle, temping of things to come. Once again, he wondered why he had been alone for so many years.

She listened and smiled and soon purred like a happy cat. Her forehead relaxed and the furrow in her brow went away. He hesitated at a coma and she interjected in a quiet, whispery voice, "I like this story." He leaned over and kissed her, seated himself again, and resumed reading.

Suddenly, they heard a loud, nerve-wracking *SLAP!* as a large, wet, beach towel was slung over the tall, wooden fence near the outside of their bathroom wall.

She sat straight up in the tub. The furrow immediately appeared in her brow and she stood up, still beautiful, but rigid. She stepped out of the tub and grabbed up her robe on the way out, leaving a trail of water and wet footprints, mumbling as she pounded away. Nic was left sitting in the chair by the tub of warm water, Hemingway in Paris, and all sorts of things that could have happened from it, dead in his lap.

He went into the den. The back door was open and she was standing in it, looking out to the tall, wooden fence. He heard The Eagles proclaim out of the boom box next door, "Wel-come to the Hotel Ca-li-for-nia, such a lovely place," such a lovely face.' "

He did not know what to do, but he knew he had to do something. He stood in the dark looking at her in the doorway. As her damp skin at her throat where her collarbones met glistened in the soft light, the Eagles said, "You can check out any time you like, but you can ne-vah leave."

The next morning, he walked her to her car. As he came back around to the deck, he could see the neighbor's skimming-net pole over the tall, wooden fence. The pole wagged and jerked, stupidly, in the air as his neighbor skimmed southern pine straw and hardwood leaves off the surface of his dark, cool, inviting pool.

Nic walked over to the pickle bucket, stood upon it, and looked over the fence.

The neighbor looked up, surprised that Nic could somehow see over but he did not ask how. Nic's face was barely above the horizontal plane of the top.

"Hey," neighbor said.

"Hi," Nic said.

The neighbor was at the other end of the pool and he kept skimming where he was. *Is he going to take a minute and come over here?* Nic thought.

He did not. It made Nic feel awkward.

The boom box was on, playing the local early morning talk show. It was not loud, but it was distracting. It made it difficult for Nic to talk.

"I need to talk with you," Nic said.

"What's that?" the neighbor said.
"I need to talk with you," Nic said again.

"Ok," the neighbor said, "What about?"

"Well," Nic started, "Hey, can you turn the radio off for a minute?"

Neighbor put the pole down and walked over to the radio and turned it down, but not all the way. The neighbor looked at him from afar. Nic felt as though the neighbor knew he was standing on a pickle bucket and still had to hold his head back to see over while he balanced and tried to talk, and that the neighbor took advantage of this to create an edge for himself.

"What were you saying?" the neighbor asked, having to talk loudly because he was so far away.

"Well," Nic started, then the pickle bucket moved a little and he looked down, "I was wondering if you all could stop hanging things over the fence, you know, towels, nets, anything, really?"

The neighbor just looked at him.

"Can you hear me?" Nic said after a couple of beats.

"Yea," neighbor said.

Nic stood there waiting for the neighbor to say more. He did not. It became awkward. Nic said, "You've been married a while and you know how it is. It bothers my wife."

Finally, neighbor said, "They don't hurt the fence or anything."

Nic was taken aback that the neighbor even dared to introduce this or any counter. Nic immediately knew that if he acquiesced in any way, he would be agreeing to neighbor's point.

Nic felt a cold chill go over him. The pickle bucket shifted. Nic had to look down again. When he looked back up, the neighbor had his hands on his waist as if he were some muddy, bloody quarterback late in the fourth quarter demonstrating to the other side by the pose he struck that he was determined to win, even if it went into overtime. He was looking straight into Nic's eyes, making it clear that any further comment was Nic's to make, so far as he was concerned.

Nic did not know the neighbor well enough to know if he was simply crafty like an attorney, or if, maybe, he was very smart and was trying- and maybe he just did -to play a gambit in a game only he understood, a game designed to disarm Nic and determine the ultimate outcome, right then and there.

Crap, Nic thought, *this guy could be one of those decision-tree expert-type guys like we had in Virginia in graduate school, and my throat could already be cut, and I don't even know it, yet.*

As if in Judo, Nic immediately decided to back out and return later.

"Hey, you know," Nic held his head back and said, "I'm standing on a pickle bucket and I'm going to bust my butt and it is early and we both have to get going. Let's talk about this later."

Neighbor just looked at him. Nic noted he did not acknowledge his comment; he did not verbally agree or shake his head, affirmatively or negatively. He just stood there with his hands on his hips like a real...cool...customer.

Nic stepped off the bucket and went up on the deck and cleaned his shoes on the mat and went inside. He closed the door and leaned against it. It was dark inside. He found himself standing very, very still and holding his breath, listening for the neighbor to walk across his deck and come to the door. When he realized he was doing this, he shook his head and looked at the cat sitting on the couch. The cat watched him, wryly. Nic laughed and said to himself, *Shake it off, man,* like he and his teammates would say to each other after an error long ago on the baseball diamond.

Nic wrote until lunch. As he walked out to his car in the driveway because the garage was full of antiques, he saw police boy drive by in his cruiser. *Guess he's coming home for lunch,* Nic thought.

Nic waived. Police boy did not.

Nic stopped in the driveway just before the street to pick up a pine limb that had fallen. He put it by the street and looked up. Neighbor was outside as police boy got out of his cruiser with his Glock, radio, and ridiculous, Marine-style, haircut. Father and son had some words Nic could not hear. They both looked at Nic.

Nic waived. They did not. They turned and went inside.

To serve and protect, little boy, Nic said under his breath as the cold, pickle bucket chill came back over him.

Nic went into the bigger, contiguous city to have lunch with his editor.

Nic and his wife walked past neighbor's house late that afternoon on their way to the park.

They walked the trail for two miles. They watched a couple play tennis. She told him she had not played since high school and that she wanted to try it again. He told her he already had two tennis rackets and she could use one to see if she still liked the game before they bought another for her.

They walked back. As they approached the neighbor's house, Nic could see he and his wife outside. His wife went in. The neighbor looked at Nic. Nic waived. The neighbor turned and continued to wash his pickup.

Nic went out to the grocery store around nine that night for things needed the next morning. He finished his shopping and as he walked up to his car in the parking lot, police boy drove by in his cruiser, slowly. Nic nodded. Police boy looked at him. He might have nodded very slightly. Nic could not tell.

Nic returned, and as he walked back around to the deck and put his hand on the doorknob, he looked out to the tall, wooden fence and there were towels and the net on the fence, again. He could see the pool lights through the cracks. He could hear people talking. He took the groceries into the kitchen.

He thought about things being on the fence. He walked back out the back door and up to the fence, reached, and threw the towels, one by one, then the net, over to the ground on the other side.

He heard the conversations around the pool stop but he did not hesitate as he turned and went back inside.

As he prepared breakfast the next morning, she came through in her summer robe. She was nude underneath. He could see the curves of her body. She saw him looking and said, "Stop it, I'm late," and she ran to the guest bathroom and locked the door. He rattled the knob. He heard her turn on the water. He thought of her stepping into the shower, her naked body, her beautiful skin, her fragrant soap, and he went to the kitchen and came back with an ice pick and stuck it in the hole in the knob and opened the door. He took his clothes off and got into the shower with her.

He walked her to her car. He walked back around the house and stepped back upon the deck. He felt someone looking at him. He looked up. His neighbor was peering over the top of the fence. "You threw our towels and net off our fence into my yard last night," the neighbor said.

"You sure are a talker all of a sudden. What happened?" Nic said.

Neighbor continued to look at him. Nic guessed he was trying to think what to say.

"I asked you politely," Nic said as he walked into their house and shut the door.

That night, Nic made a dinner of a simple, coarse salad with homemade vinaigrette dressing, snap beans lightly cooked in a small amount of butter, and red fish he caught the previous year in Louisiana in the brackish waters. He called the dinner French because she was now reading the Hemingway in Paris book. "French cuisine my eye," she said with a cute laugh.

"Contrare," he protested.

He put the dishes away and he got the tennis racquets. They went for a walk down to the park and watched some people play and then hit some, themselves: "You are doing very well," he said. "Your muscles are remembering."

They returned and showered and she sat on the couch in her robe and got her book and stretched out her long, silky legs, down the couch, putting her feet in his lap. She read aloud while he applied lotion to her legs and feet and worked it in with great attention.

He massaged her feet at points he learned from a reflexology chart. When he hit right, she would stop reading and moan with pleasure. "Keep reading," he would say, "Don't leave Papa stranded in the café. They do not have much coal left for the fireplace. It is getting late and is chilly in Paris." She rolled her eyes.

At bedtime, she went to their bedroom first. He looked out the back door and over to the tall, wooden fence and the towels and net were there. He quickly walked out and threw all of them onto the ground on the neighbor's side.

"What were you doing?" she asked as she saw the back door open when she came back for a glass of water.

"Nothing," he said. She knew better. She looked at the tall, wooden fence. There were no towels; no net; no anything.

She looked at him. "What?" he said.

She walked away. Just before the hall to the bedroom, she stopped, un-sashed her robe, took it off and threw it over her shoulder like it were a car coat and she were in Times Square.

She turned slightly so he could see her left breast peaking around, "You coming to bed, Hemingway?"

While she slept, Nic stared at the ceiling and thought about how long it had been since he talked with Andre' Dubus III. He tried to remember the details of the story in Dubus's "The House of Sand and Fog" but he could not. He remembered there was controversy about the house and the living in it, as there is always conflict in good literature.

He recalled having dinner with Andre and Steve Yarbrough in Oxford. He thought about how Andre told the audience at the Larry Brown Conference on the Book, about how he and Larry discovered they both loved carpentry. And, that they wrote and mailed long, paper letters back and forth about their respective projects.

Nic thought about the tall, wooden fence and the risks of controversy and conflict it presented, and about carpentry. Though a fence is more simple than the houses he and Larry were building, he wondered what Andre would say about the fence, and about all the humanity heating up.

Maybe I'll write him a paper letter, he thought.

The next afternoon, she came home and there were pickup trucks in the driveway and two cars on the street. She walked around on the stepping stones. When she rounded the corner, she saw Nic and some men sitting at the picnic table on the deck, looking down at large, architectural-type drawings, unrolled and held down at the corners by pieces of brick, a tape measure, and a hammer.

Behind them, was a new, taller, stronger, wooden fence.

Nic looked up from the discussion and smiled when he saw her. Her mouth fell open. A look of surprise crossed her face.

"What is this?" she said.

"A new, wooden fence," he said. "The old one sagged. And, it was too short for what we need, now."

"But, you didn't say anything to me," she said.

"I wanted to surprise you," he said. "Come here, Look at these drawings," he said.

She was trying to be mad about him not telling her. She looked down and saw the drawings. The colors made her feel placid. Her bubbling anger and resentment melted away like ice sculptures in August. "Oh, it's beautiful," she said.

"Yes, but which one, or what of anything else would you like?" he asked. "We can paint anything you desire on the fence, or leave it blank."

Nic looked at his watch and thought, *Neighbor should be home any minute now.* He heard the neighbor's back door open and close.

Yep, Nic thought, *game on.*

Nic turned and looked at the new, taller, wooden fence and though the boards were thicker and the cracks tighter, he could see the neighbor's shadow as he was trying to look through.

"Howdy neighbor," Nic shouted, "Come on over and take a look."

Neighbor stepped upon the deck. Nic extended his hand. Neighbor shook in an obligatory manner.

Nic said, "The city surveyor recorded this new fence as being one, whole foot inside our property line."

Neighbor looked around at the fence and saw a No Trespassing sign. He looked at Nic. Nic looked at him and nodded. "Trespassing is $500,"

Nic said as he nodded, again.

Neighbor raised his finger in the air to say something. Nic shook his head side to side, ever so slightly.

Neighbor's finger went down, slowly, like air oozing out of an old tire.

"You want an Arnold Palmer?" Nic asked his neighbor.

"What?" the neighbor said. He was angry but not showing it. For a second, he thought Nic was saying 'Arnold Palmer' as an euphemism for knuckle sandwich or something like that they'd said as kids and he had forgotten.

"Arnold Palmer," Nic said. "Half iced tea, half lemonade. They call it an Arnold Palmer." Nic reached over, poured him a glass, and extended. "Would you like some?"

Neighbor took the glass. Nic raised his and said: "Here's to a good, long life as neighbors."

Three days later, Nic was cooking dinner for her in the afternoon. He heard her car door close, followed by silence, as she went to the mailbox. He saw her blonde hair through the window as she rounded the corner. Predictably, she bent down to touch, and tend her flowers. When she was done, she stepped, and froze, and gazed toward the fence Nic built.

Nic opened the back door. Two, tortuous towels, and the blue, injurious net were hanging over the fence.

Nic took the digital camera from the shelf near the door, walked out, and shot pictures.

The neighbor was at work the next day. He was told he had a visitor.

The Constable was standing in the lobby. Neighbor and The Constable went to First Baptist Church together, were in the same Sunday School class, and both played softball on the church team.

Neighbor said, "Hey Jim, what's up? You going to be there tonight?"

"Yes, Jim said, but that's not why I'm here. Sorry, you've been served," and he handed neighbor an envelope.

Nic beat the neighbor in court almost before it started. The Judge ordered the neighbor to write Nic a $500 check. And, another to the court for $50. Court fees.

Nic was in the front yard the next day and the neighbor came out into his own front yard. Neighbor opened his mouth-- Nic cut him off. "Look, man," Nic said, "we can get along and maybe even be friends, but not if you are going to run over my wife and me. I'm serious. You will be writing $500 checks until the cows come home."

Later that night, Nic was reading in bed, waiting for her. She came in, hung her robe on the back of the door, climbed in bed and snuggled up, leaning into him as though they were falling from a plane, together, and he wore the parachute. He could smell her hair.

"What are you reading?" she asked.

"Faulkner," he said.

"I thought Barry Hannah told you to not read Faulkner because you needed to write more economically and Faulkner would ruin you."

"He did," Nic said.

She was quiet but Nic could hear the question.

"This is a collection of short stories. I think Barry was talking about novels. That was two years ago. I still haven't picked up a Faulkner novel. But, I see what he is doing in these short stories; plus, I like the way his characters talk. I have known people like these Faulkner characters. People in the Mississippi country side, doing the best they can with little resources."

Nic read to himself. She was quiet for a few minutes.

"So, why didn't you tell me you were going to replace the fence?" she said as calmly as an undertaker.

The room fell silent.

"You mad?" he asked.

"I don't know; hurt, I guess; I guess I'm hurt. It scares me that you just did it. Why didn't you tell me?" she said.

"I didn't want you to worry or get involved," he said.

"Involved?" she said. "I've lived here for years and we…"

"Please," he interrupted, "please do not say that."

"Say what?" she asked.

"That *he* and you built the fence and you worked overtime and you all paid for it and blah, blah, blah, that's what, I'm sick of hearing that, I can't hear it anymore, and now I shouldn't have to..."

She did not move. She did not say anything.

"Look," he said, "the whole thing with the fence and the neighbor was probably going to grow into a big mess. I told him you didn't like it but he didn't care. I told him weeks ago, as I was standing on a pickle bucket, about to break my neck, and he didn't even respond. Moving of the fence to create trespass was the only gambit, probably, but I'da done it, anyway, because I had to build you a fence!"

"A pickle bucket?" she said.

"It's a long story," he said.

"Seems like it," she said.

"What about the trespassing and all that mess?" she said.

"What mess?" he said.

"The court mess," she said.

"There is no court mess: it's over; it was over before it started," he said.

"He had to pay $500," she said.

"He sure did," he said, "and he'll have to do it as many times as he has to before he gets the message."

"Do you think that's right?" she said.

"Do I think what is right? Do you want to live with his crime of junk hanging over the fence, visible in our yard? You must be joking?" he said.

She was quiet.

He leaned up on his elbow and looked at her. "Look, I want you to listen to me. I love you very, very much. You are the absolute love of my life. I have missed opportunity before and I have regrets. Thank goodness I did not miss you. This might seem selfish, but I want to live with you, really live, I do not want to miss a thing, I want to live peacefully with everyone and experience new things with you, all the time."

He looked at her. She started to say something. "I love you," he said. "I love you, I love you, I love you. It should be enough. It really should be enough; it, and that I took action for you, for us."

She smiled.

It was dark as they drifted off to sleep. He could hear and feel her breathing. He felt her breasts on his back and once again, he wondered why he had been alone for so long.

"You awake?" he asked.

"Yes," she said.

"Will you do me a favor?" he said.

"What?" she said.

"Will you tell your sister and other people that I had the new fence built for you; that I paid for it; that I thought of the mural and found the artist; that you wanted the Queen's Rose Garden in London painted on the fence and that I had it done, just so, for you, please?"

NOTE: This story is about how a pet, even a kitten, can change a man. Even my he-man readers like this story. They see much in it, much about life and the heart. Such is what I was after.

"The Shrubs of Kilimanjaro"

My wife is gorgeous. She is downright steamy. She made my knees buckle the moment I met her, 30 something years ago.

She looks like a cross between Marilyn Monroe and Kim Bassinger. One of our neighbors, who was a WWII aviator, told me one day as he stared at her like all men do, that for men his age, she looks like a living, *breathing* Vargas girl. I laughed and said, "Well, maybe we should name a Bomber after her."

He quipped, "I already thought of that."

So, my Vargas girl reclined on the couch in her thin, summer robe-- completely nude underneath, save a pair of cute, footie socks --with her gorgeous legs stretched out for two seat cushions as I looked at her and thought how I was going to ease that robe off her lovely frame when the sun went down, and about how we would love, and how after, we'd coil together like two, nautical ropes until we succumbed to sleep on the soft, fresh sheets she keeps on our bed. She says they are Egyptian cotton, one thousand thread count.

She held the tiny kitten to her chest and rubbed the top of his little head. He's at the stage his skull reminds me of a ping-pong ball. His head is so small, she rubs him with the tip of her index finger. She talks baby talk as she rubs.

She informed me the other day she named him Wolfie because at his current stage of development, he looks like a little werewolf in the face. Not scary, no. Cute, a cute, baby werewolf, if you know what I mean.

She asked me what I thought about the name. It didn't matter. Wolfie it was. I knew it. Asking me was a formality. It was her way of informing me. Wolfie it is.

She is hooked. She first said he would be an outside cat. Now she is thinking aloud about declawing to protect her leather sofa.

This whole kitten thing started two days ago when she called me on the phone in the late afternoon, proclaiming there were four kittens, out in the open, on the ground amongst the shrubs at the back of our house. I asked, "Are you sure?" Duh.

The reason I asked is because while I love my wife and will not live without her, she is one of those women who the dark forces for chaos surely watch all the time for terrestrial opportunities. Man oh man, things stay stirred up.

What I mean is that even on a *light day,* she continually proves: she can wake up, loose one or more pieces of jewelry; misplace, drop, or break her cell phone; run off the other side of the road in her car and drag her driver-side mirror off on a speed limit sign; on the way to work, have a disagreement on her cell phone with a co-worker that escalates into a full-blown, HR, political incident by the end of business; spill beverage on her skirt she just sprung out of the cleaners so she'll look good giving a speech at an off-site conference in a big, downtown hotel; then, 'accidentally' leave her purse at the hotel after the conference and have to go back to get it, after she has called and instructed me to phone the hotel and direct the staff to guard the bag as she carves through traffic in her silver, M3 convertible like Emmitt Smith slashing through NFL defenses-- the Bimmer's SMG transmission *screeeeammming!* as she slaps the FI shift paddles like Hans Stuck at Nurburgring. And, mind you, all this *after* she left our house that morning with *every* light on and 2 TV's blaring at high volume, so, she says, her Chihuahua will not get lonely.

You see what I'm saying?

So, I was hoping maybe, just maybe, she was mistaken and there were *not* four kittens in the shrubs because I had to go out of town overnight that afternoon and I was up to my eyeballs in work commitments until the weekend. It was only Tuesday. Plus, I knew in my bones, in the experienced husband way, that this thing, if true, was going to be another situation of which she would take ownership, but for which I would be responsible and accountable.

So, I arrived home in the late afternoon the day my wife called to tell me the cat stork had delivered four baby kittens in our shrubs. I walked around the corner of our house. Vargas girl was leaning over the bushes, looking in on the kittens.

I have never been involved with newborn kittens. If I had been first on the scene, I would have guessed there was a bird's nest full of babies in the bushes. The kittens more or less chirped: Meu, meu, meu, meu, a half second apart, over and over again, times four. They sounded like an itsy-bitsy, French ambulance, way off in the distance. For some reason, the sound made me think of Zinnemann's 1973 film, "The Day of The Jackel."

Two looked like they needed resurrecting; a third, Mayo Clinic, stat; the fourth, later to be known as Wolfie, looked like he might have a dog's chance, no pun intended.

We had our children long ago. They are off on their own except to come back on occasion to hit me up for a bridge loan that usually ends up being just a bridge; so, it had been a long time since I thought of or had to deal with the utter helplessness of a sure enough, new born.

Therefore, the kittens shocked me. They were tiny. I mean tiny. Each could fit in my hand with room to spare.

To be honest, they kinda freaked me out, like *rewind and make them go away,* freak me out. But, this was not TiVo. This was real life. I was in neck deep.

I said to my wife, "Hey, you're the one with the scrubs and the white coat saving people's lives in the ER."

Ooo. What a dumb, man thing to say. She had mentally clocked out. She gave me the look to prove it. I thought to myself, *It's my move, like it or not.*

Time constraints, pressure, and the dagger look from Marilyn

Monroe, made me get that two minute in the 4th quarter, I'm the quarterback, and we're down by six, feeling. I could feel my lungs dilate as adrenaline rolled through by bloodstream.

"I'll be right back."

On the way to the store, I called my sister. She is a true, mammal expert.

A family of 8 could retire to Fiji and all live to be ninety years old on the dough my sister has blown on animals and animal supplies. She is a human nurse who should have been a veterinarian.

Surprisingly, she alluded to the 'bash their little heads in' strategy, predicated on, she said, those kittens were days old with no mother in sight. Consequently, sister said, we were looking at a feed by eye dropper situation for several weeks. She also made it abundantly clear to me that there was no room in her inn, nor, in case I was thinking about it, was there even a manger on her property.

Crap!! *I don't have time for this,* I say to myself as I stood in the store. I bought breast milk substitute, a little bitty bottle that looked like it came in a baby-doll kit, and one of those big, clear, plastic bins with a lid. We didn't need the lid.

My wife was still standing by the bushes when I returned. She had a spectator look on her face. She had abdicated. *Crap,* I thought.

"My sister pointed out," I said like we were really going to analyze this, "that since the Mama cat is apparently a neighborhood, ho-harlot-swinger," I said, trying to be funny but she didn't laugh, "we're gonna have to bottle feed until they get up to speed."

Kim Bassinger looked at me, flatly, flat like a nylon tire in an old, dusty barn.

Say something, I'm thinking. She didn't.

Crap, woman! I think to myself as I look in her eyes, searching for a crack in her resolve. *Jump into action with stethoscope, paddles, say 'clear' and shock 'em like on T.V., hec, intubate, something, do something.* She just stared at me.

"You could go inside," I said feeling queasy about what I'd have to do if she said Ok, "and let me take care of this. My sister said it's an option."

Wife continued to look at me. This time with moral indignation, as though I had proposed hiring a hit man to gun down my mother-in-law in cold blood.

"My sister asked me," I said, "if I knew how many cats there are in the world?" I paused, "Suggesting," I gently lobbed, "a little population thinning would not be an entirely bad thing."

Vargas girl looked at me like I was Hitler.

"Ooooo-Kay," I said in resignation.

We lined the bin with bath towels. Then, using small hand towels, we picked up the kittens, put them in the bin, and took them inside.

Three of the kittens looked like aliens. They really bothered me. I had never dealt with newborn kittens. Wolfie looked a little better, though not much, but you could see he had the best chance. At least I could tell he was a kitten.

First thing I did inside was search the internet to figure how old they were so I could know where I stood. I immediately found a site that looked like my sister could be the owner. It appeared to be the location for all things of kitten-hood.

From pictures and descriptions, I deduced we were dealing with 3 to 5 day old kittens.

I mixed the substitute milk. We managed to get them fed. They hit the milk like a horde of skinny humanity, pouncing on a bag of UN rice dropped from a C-130.

I found myself being moved to having a lump in my throat by the innate reaching for life by the vagabond kittens, especially the one later called Wolfie. He was hell bent on living. You could tell even then.

Against what seemed like invisible cellophane being pushed down upon them to smother and quash their lives, they pushed back, gasping for food, air, and a chance for life-- for dignity, and to be taken seriously --and, to take their place in this cruel world.

I progressed quickly from process manager, to advocate, to cheerleader: *Come on!,* I found myself thinking while maintaining a stone exterior, *don't you give up!,* I'd think to myself about them, especially Wolfie.

My wife was drawn in, too, by a mixture of love and professional pride. In one iffy moment, she exclaimed to one of the Martian kittens as she held him up, blew into his face and shook him, "Don't you die on me!"

I left that night. A friend took the kittens the next day while I was working out of town and my wife was at the hospital, doctoring on humans. Two died during the morning, the third passed into cat heaven in the late afternoon.

Wolfie made it.

The next day, remembering nutrition experiments using cats during the 1930's and 40's, I ordered the best feline total body support in the world for Wolfie. $16, plus $25 for overnight shipping. This was a stat situation. I was down with what had developed into our 'Bring Wolfie Through' campaign.

Feline support came in. I learned to put a tablet in a paper towel and crush it with a thick, table spoon against the chopping block. Then, I'd thump the powder off the towel into the substitute milk concoction, ready for the small bottle or syringe.

I learned the hard way to warm the bottle or syringe under running, warm to hot water. I did not do it the one time it took me to learn and Wolfie, being hungry, gulped down the cold preparation as I pushed the plunger. He shook all over with a chill so hard, it looked like he was seizing. It scared me. I thought I was loosing him and my ER doc wife was not around. So, as she had done, I screamed out, without thinking, "Don't you die on me!"

Wolfie was downright inspiring. He was like me: A man making his way and having to insist on respect in the midst of the harshness of life and the warp and woof of living.

I went from a man who knew nothing of cats and kittens, to a fellow who did not care what Wolfie was, but that I respected him for his fight for life and significance.

Wolfie, though he weighed less than a tennis ball, was renewing pieces of my courage to live large I did not know I had lost.

My wife and I were drawn together more strongly by our mutual commitment to Wolfie's survival. We'd lie in bed and let Wolfie wobble around upon and between us, practicing, I figured, on his brain, nerves and muscles coordination.

I was fascinated watching him hold on to level ground as for dear life, with claws at full extension, as he made his way around the bed, and us, like a crazed man compelled to move with no particular destination, but on the move, nevertheless, as if in a land rush, putting claim on as much terrain as possible, simply by having been there.

I never searched a kitten development schedule on the internet, so I do not know. But, it seemed to me, that like human babies early on, Wolfie could not see far away. But, it occurred to me, that to see far away didn't matter much when you were always dodging the angel of death, close in.

Nature reflects Wisdom.

Now, after a time, I could tell he could see me from the foot. He would hesitate and look at me with acknowledgment, his length of vision having increased.

Wolfie did not owe me. But, his looking me in the eye made me feel the way I felt the day my son crossed the podium at college graduation and looked up at me and gave me a big thumbs up, along with a nod, that I knew was his unspoken, man to man, signal of thanks and appreciation.

Amazing.

I was surprised that the look of this tiny kitten and the smile and thumbs up from my son after completing a $45,000 college degree gave me the same feeling. *I must be getting old*, I thought.

Wolfie made it through the valley of the shadow of death. I'd sit at the kitchen table and watch him drink milk from a bowl. He looked like a miniature lion in the Serengeti at a lone pool of water.

He would finish and stand with all four legs a little wider than his shoulders against his bulging girth, full of milk.

He would look at me, deeply, for about five seconds. I would have this feeling he was saying to me, "I know you. You helped me out of the bushes. I will not forget!"

My wife left early one morning. I had the TV's and unneeded lights off. The blinds open.

Quiet.

Still.

I sat at the kitchen table, drank green tea and honey, read pieces of Hemingway, Hannah, Carver, McCarthy, and my dear Yarbrough, and watched Wolfie drink milk, laced with body support I bought for him and had shipped, overnight.

He stood like the fictitious leopard of Kilimanjaro. He finished, stood straightly and stared at me. I thought to myself as I looked at him, *the kitten from the shrubby ghetto made it. In spite of the fact his mother was a neighborhood tramp and his father unknown, he possesses regality; I think Hemingway would call it 'a good pride.' I do not know why. I bet he would.*

I returned late that evening and sat at the table for a few minutes and watched Wolfie explore. I turned on the radio in the kitchen and started dinner. Making dinner for Vargas girl soothes me and gives me pleasure, especially when I hit upon something she really enjoys.

I finished cooking. I set it aside and waited for her.

I poured milk into Wolfie's bowl. I sat in the floor close to him, cross legged like an American Indian in front of his teepee. I watched him drink like the Lion. I picked him up when he was full. He purred and rubbed his head in my chest. "You noble cat, you," I said to him.

My wife came in. We had dinner. Then, we went to the den and I read my latest short story to her as the ceiling fan turned, slowly as if we were in Key West.

She listened. She enjoyed.

She took a bath.

After, she was clean and soft. She lay on the bed, nude under her short, summer robe, reclined on a beautiful, gold pillow, like a queen. She smelled like jasmine.

I did not say a word. I took out expensive lotion I bought for her and began to rub into her feet, then her legs, massaging her muscles deeply like a masseur at an exclusive resort.

I told her my name was Hans. She laughed.

I worked intently without looking up, appreciating her gorgeous legs that reminded me of statues in Rome.

I rubbed the lotion into her hands and fingers with great effort and detail as if the lotion was Frankincense brought to me by wise men from the other side of the globe.

Then, I moved up her arms and did the same. Her robe fell loose. She yielded and rolled over, and I rubbed deeply into her back, down to the small part, and then to her beautiful, heart-shaped bottom and down her legs and back to the soles of her feet where it all began.

I picked up each foot, gently bending each leg at the knee. I lovingly worked deeply into her foot, therapeutically rotated her ankles and occasionally looking up to admire her magnificent figure.

I thought she was asleep. I covered her with her robe. I was at the door. With her face still in her pillow, she asked, "Where' you going?"

I thought. I felt.

I said, "I do not say it enough, but I want you to know, you are a very good and valuable woman, and I love you, madly."

Without moving, she responded, "What about beautiful, do you think I am beautiful?"

"No," I said, "You are far more than beautiful."

"How far?" she asked.

"You are stunning, exquisite, and gorgeous. You still make my knees buckle."

She said, "I'll find out later what has happened to you. I think Wolfie has made you a better man."

"May be," I said.

"Right now," she raised her head and looked at me, "Why don't you come back to our bed and show me how stunning, exquisite, and gorgeous you believe I am."

I now like cats.

125

NOTE: This story placed high in a contest. I don't remember exactly how I thought of this story. Except, I did go to a junk yard one day, and I do remember being impacted by the truths that ended up in the story. I am a car guy. I have spent time in moonlight shops. I think I connected some dots that had been in my head a long time to make the story. This story might make you cry near the end as it makes you picture your loved ones in peril. Finishes with subtle, but true, inner conflict of heart.

"Volvos and Water Moccasins"

My name is Nicolas Horn. I was born and I live in Mississippi. I make my living in outside sales. I read and write fiction. I want to write fiction for a living. It is powerful because when good, it reveals truths of the human heart in conflict with itself. Faulkner said so.

I am a car enthusiast. I love BMW's and have owned a few. I have owned several Volvos over the years and I have one now. I need to get rid of it. I need a new perspective. I'm gonna sell it shortly.

I've probably spent half my life in various import car repair shops run by a guy or guys who moonlight after hours of working full time at the local dealership. I've scoured junk yards in recent years, too-- something I never thought of myself doing in my younger years --looking for air mass meters, alternators, turbo chargers, OEM hub caps, you name it.

This is the plight of those of us who buy the used cars of cardiologists, oncologists, attorneys and so forth because we do not make the income necessary to buy the expensive cars we love and after which we lust from the dealerships when the cars are spanking new. Sickness, drugs, and suing buy many of the new and expensive European cars in America. We buy them used and years old, and we lovingly clean the leather seats and wax the metal, and we change the expensive, synthetic oil and German-made filters ourselves and take the cars to club meetings where they are admired by others who, like the second -or third -or forth-hand owners we are, truly appreciate the automotive manifestations of the European mind.

Much of the time I've spent at moonlight shops has not been spent productively, that is if you do not count all the reading or listening to good fiction and non-fiction I always have in my car, and the writing I've done since I started writing, like I am doing right now, as I stand at the trunk of my current Euro car and use the lid as a desk while the sun beams down on me in August, again on a Saturday, while waiting on the guy to get here to fix my car for less than the dealership would cost, and for as little as I can get him down to and he still make a profit.

It's 9:16 AM and he was supposed to be here at 9:00 but he called to tell me he had to take his son 'across town' and would be about 30 minutes. That was at 9:00, and after I texted him at 8:30 informing that I was at the shop on the improbable chance he wanted to start earlier. 'Across town:' I wonder what that really means in terms of time?

God works in mysterious ways. He is not cruel, the Bible informs us, but he can put the screws to you in His own way. Of course, I know Adam and Eve made the wrong choice of their own free will and catalyzed this mess, but as the kids say now, 'I'm just saying' because if you want to be straight about it, the problem with Adam's and Eve's bone headed move is that they took us all into a world of thorns, thistles, pain and sorrows.

When I get to heaven, the Apostle Paul, Granddaddy, Moses, Ronald Reagan, Elvis, and all the other notables people say they want to talk with immediately upon arrival are gonna have to hang on a minute while I go find Adam and Eve and go upside Adam's head and give Eve a good, Southern bawlin' out. Matter of fact, if they happen to be in conference with Jesus Himself when I show up, I think I will ask Jesus if he would excuse us for a minute while I have a little chat with A and E. "Lord," I'd say, "I know time doesn't matter anymore, but could I interrupt and talk with A and E in private for, Oh, 3 minutes on the old clock? Thank you, Lord, I really appreciate it, and in the meantime until I can express my full gratitude, may I say I sincerely appreciate all you've done for me and I'm very happy to be here because I know you did the work to get me here."

But back to what I was saying before the A and E detour, God puts the screws to you and so on, and it seems to me when you know that is happening, you just hunker down and look for some silver lining. Sometimes you get mad about your situation, and when that's the case you have to stop and more forcefully make yourself look around for that silver lining, trusting all the while that in contrast to the way you feel, it is there, somewhere. The other thing is if you feel your situation is correlated to something you need to square up with the Lord about, you gotta do that, and you have to understand that squaring up probably does not mean everything gets prefect all of a sudden: Gears might have been kicked into motion on the human side that must grind out like in a music box 'till the tune is over. That's back to the A and E thing, but we will not go into that again. But, as an extreme example, what I am saying is that it is like if you murder someone and there is a body and witnesses and you did do it and are convicted and go to jail, squaring up in the cell is not gonna spring you until the gears of the human toll run down. Another example would be if you have a baby by your neighbor who is not your wife but you do have a wife and your neighbor has a husband, well, there's the baby: The baby won't go away, except through, for example, some form of tort, and that throws you back to the murder and jail thing till the human, time-space gears run down. Like a I said, I'd like to kick A and E in their respective behinds 'till their noses bleed but we won't go there right now because it is premature and we have some things to talk about in the here and now.

So my plight because I have not figured out how to make enough money to buy newer cars and drop them off at the dealership for their *so many miles service* while I go to the club and play tennis has me standing out here in front of trunk of my used, Euro car using the trunk deck for a desk in the sunshine writing this memoir with a pen on a legal pad. I usually write on a laptop, but mine is old and the battery does not last long enough for me to go mobile and use it if there is not an electrical outlet handy, not to mention I couldn't see the screen for the glare out here anyway, but on the other hand, I read Hemingway sometimes wrote in cafés in Paris in the 20's, and so this writing with a pen thing has me feeling, rightly or wrongly, like I'm really being a writer. Now that I think about it, that J.K. Rowling lady wrote the first Harry Potter in a coffee shop in or around London with pen and paper and a hungry baby in tow. See, this pen and pad thing on the back of the car trunk has a silver lining.

But, the bigger silver lining about my whole car situation lies all around me, and I did not completely see it for years until some time after I started actively writing. The silver lining around moonlight repair shops and junkyards is that if and only if you are writer of fiction or maybe a country music song writer, there are stories to be written and songs to be sung about stories you can begin to imagine by looking through the windows and in the trunks of the cars at all the stuff generated by the living of real people engaged in the struggles of life.

Concerning the cars outside the Euro moonlight shop, people leave them there for months or years or as long as they guy will let them get away with it. It is usually because they blew a motor or some other major thing that costs a lot and they cannot swing it because life is sucking money out of them every day because of inflation and such, and so their car just sits there like an athlete with a pulled hamstring- they look normal but they can't go.

The junkyard cars are there because they blew something too expensive to fix that rendered them more valuable as parts cars like the mechanical equivalent of organ donors, or they are there because of a debilitating auto accident, but they are still valuable as a donor of parts not broken or destroyed by the crash.

Story is what the writer is or should be concerned about. When I look into the windows or the trunks of the cars sitting quietly on gravel or sometimes grass at the moonlight shop, I see things of the stories of various lives I imagine Ray Carver would also see when put in combination with things of observation he would already have in his mind about people trying to make it as best they can on their little patch of the globe.

I see items like Bibles, school schedules, electric bills, water bills, credit card statements, bank statements, check books, hats, socks, shirts, blouses, pants, and skirts, bras and panties but not necessarily together indicating each was, on different occasions, put in the car for a change of clothes, the latest Joel Osteen shiny happy book ironically promising in a round about way that if you do this or that to get you favor with God you will have enough money to buy yourself a new Euro Car and whatever else you want, magazines, coffee cups, a baton for twirling (?), shoes— lots of shoes –Sunday School books, oh, and numbers of CD's, tapes, envelopes containing fraudulent claims by lawyer firms masquerading as collection agencies, paperback fiction, hard cover fiction, non-fiction books in every configuration, combs, brushes, pens and pencils, and many other things, some surprising, that I cannot recall at this moment.

Junk yards and junk yard cars are a little different to me: many of them encased dead or injured until they limped away or were extracted and put into ambulance or coroner's wagon. Like the undertaker eating a sandwich during an autopsy, I guess most of the junk yard workers don't think so much of this because it is a job like any other they use for money to buy things and to support their families, but if you ask them, they'll tell you they do see strange things from time to time.

I went to this junkyard a few weeks ago to look for some hoses for a '92 940 Volvo Turbo. We found a wrecked '95: '95 940's have much of the same equipment as '92 940's.

Volvos have long been known to be safe. Back in the 60's or 70's, Volvo used to have a TV commercial where they would run an empty 240 off a building about 12 or more stories and after the crash and the car stopped its motion, some TV commercial actor would walk up to it and open and shut one of the doors.

The '95 with the hoses had taken a direct, 90 degree hit on the passenger side at the post between the front and back doors. It had to have been a horrendous lick because Volvos do not usually buckle all the way into the carriage, but in this case the post and doors on the passenger side were driven half way into the car such that what was left of the front passenger door was at the arm rest of the driver, and the impact and resultant crumple of the bottom of the car had rippled toward the driver and buckled up the floor under the driver's seat so that it likely drove the driver's head and neck into impact with the roof, all the while his or her inertia toward the passenger side of the car carried him or her-- according to physical law --into lateral impact with oncoming forces of steel and the passenger being pushed toward driver's side by it coming in from the passenger's right due to the side impact.

When we walked up to the black '95, I stepped ahead of the junkyard part puller kid and lifted the hood. I immediately saw the breather box at the front left corner behind the headlamps and the turbo charger tucked neatly behind and slightly below. "Yep, this is the same Turbo," I said, apprehensively looking to the two locations for the hoses: there they were and I squeezed them both and they still had much physical integrity. "Here they are," I said, "I want those, and look how in the open they are. These shouldn't cost much because they are simple hoses, and they are easy to get to and remove because they are right here on top and only clamps on each end," I said, winking at the junkyard-puller-kid.

The junkyard has the power to make you feel good through it's containment and revelation of things you need that you can participate in finding like in a scavenger hunt: I've noticed the emotion the junkyard can allow you to have as an adult is very similar to the emotion you have as a kid on an Easter Egg hunt- you are looking right at the thing and Whamo!, there it is.

As the junkyard puller stepped up with his screwdriver to easily remove the clamps from each end of the hoses, I stepped back and out of the way, standing behind him, watching and looking under the hood of the car thinking things like, 'Hmm, wonder what they'll take for that Turbo charger, it looks good and it is a Mitsubishi just like mine.'

Then I looked more deeply at the car itself and for the first time, I really saw how severely it had been damaged by the crash. I walked around to the hit side, standing in two inches of water because there had been a heavy rain the night before and the creek beyond the back wall of the junkyard was still full and straining to pull the water out of the lot. The puller-kid said from under the hood, "Keep an eye out: I saw moccasins back here this morning, but they don't bother me as much as spiders."

"They don't bother you as much as spiders," I say, "I'll never understand that, why in the world do spiders bother you more than moccasins," I asked.

He pulled up and out of from under the hood of the car to make his point as if it were very, very important for me to have the information he was about to tell me. Punching the air with his screwdriver, "You can't see spiders as easily and they can get on you and up your britches. I can crush a moccasin's head, but them spiders...hell, you can't see 'em till it's too late."

I decided not to get into a talk of the relative dangers of spiders and moccasins, particularly since I would never understand how a snake does not scare the be-jesus out of a guy, and as far as spiders go, their danger in my mind is mitigated by the fact I can step on them with my shoe, or even crush them with a rolled up newspaper. I haven't figured out how I can kill a moccasin with a Wall Street Journal. "I see what you are saying," I agreed.

Still thinking about snakes, I looked in the '95 940 Turbo from the crushed passenger's side. There were the pens and pencils on the floor, a small day-timer book, CD's, a Bible, and then I saw the blood stains all over. I did not know what they were at first because they looked like melted chocolate, but then what the stains were made of hit me.

"Are these blood stains?" I asked. Puller guy came out of the hood and walked around and looked. "Yep," he said and he handed me hose #1, "Here's one hose," he said as he turned back to the front of the car and dove back down for hose #2 like a kid in the deep end of a summer swimming pool.

Then I saw the child's shoe in the driver's seat, and hoping it was serendipity and there had been no child in this car, I looked in the back seat and mangled into the wreckage so that it looked like part of the car and you could not see it at first, was a child seat. I shot bolt up and stood there in the water and it was 98 degrees and I was sweating through my clothes so much by now I was soaked, and I looked up and all around and saw cars stacked up like a pulp wood yard that I did not notice coming in because I was on the quest for the hoses because I needed them in order to get the 940 back on the road that day.

I looked back into the car by shear force of will and I started to cry a little while the puller guy talked on about at what point they decide to put a car in the crusher. I had asked him the question before all this hit me, I had done it to myself, and he was dutifully answering it and I wished he would shut up but he would not because he did not know I was getting agonized by the mangled and the dead.

I forced myself to look back into the car and I thought of my blessed father driving and my tender mother in the passenger's seat, and my 4 year old niece with skin as of smooth clay and my handsome 8 year old nephew on the back seat, and all of them being crushed in such a ferocious impact as to cave in a Volvo and it made me bend over and put my hands on my knees and I dropped the hose in the water. The puller guy talked on, innocently.

I had this unexplainable feeling of guilt about stripping this car of usable things; I suddenly felt like I was desecrating a grave because surely one or more people died here.

I looked again as if for catharsis and I thought of my beautiful girlfriend with her exquisite, Lladro-like skin and her perfect teeth, sitting in the passenger seat talking like a record player while we ride as she always does, and all of a sudden we are hit as if by a freight train and it drives her into me with violence and we break and our organs pop and we bleed into each other and drift into eternity not having been able to say "goodbye" and "I do love you" and "it will be Ok."

Puller guy came up as if from under water, "That's it, here's the other one." "Oh," I said. He looked down at the first hose in the water. "I dropped it," I said dumbly to divert any question, and I reached down and picked it up out of the water. "Thank you," I said, "I'm sorry, I have to go right now, I have to meet a guy about work," which was not necessarily true but I said as I felt like throwing up.

As we walked out amongst the stacks of cars piled high in sections according to make, I looked purposely at them like I was some sort of inspector and didn't say anything for a while. Finally, I looked at him and asked, "You might have gotten over this, but do you still notice all the personal effects of people in these cars?"

"Yes," he said, "I notice, but we got a lot to do every day and I can't dwell on it too much, you know."

"Yes, I think I do. People died in these cars and it is kinda sad to me. I don't like to be morbid, but I can't help but think you might bump into things of the bodies of these people sometimes, like limbs and stuff."

He said, "One time there was a finger on the floorboard of a car, that's about it, but it made me feel funny."

"What did you do with the finger?" I asked.

"I picked it up and threw it out into the yard because that car had some still nice floor mats and the finger was sittin' on one of them and a man wanted the floor mats."

I said good-bye to the puller guy and went into the junk yard shack with its window A/C unit blowing hard and cold and walked up to the counter where the big guy manning the computer sat. I set the hoses down and he said, "They still good aren't they?"

"Yes," I said, "They are still good. How much?"

"Oh, $20", he said.

"Total?" I asked.

"Yea, total."

I walked out into the heat and started to put my hoses on the floor of the front passenger side. Instead, I opened the trunk and set them gently on top my golf bag.

I drove away and pushed the crushed baby seat and the story of likely death in the '95 940 Turbo from where my hoses came out of my mind.

Instead, as I felt a twinge of pride bubble up, I chose to think of how surprised my moonlight mechanic was going to be that I actually found two good hoses for a turbocharged Volvo 940 in the junkyard, and how clever he would say I am, and how much money he would say I saved versus the price of two, new, Original Equipment Manufacturer hoses from the dealership's parts department.

NOTE: Please do not dodge this story because you are not a hunter or sportsman and think it is not for you. It is a coming of age story. There is much humanity in it. And, some very powerful messages. I sincerely believe you will be happy you read it. I have a 10 year-old nephew named Matthew. I use him as the 'model' for the boy. Matthew and I did NOT take a sacred hunt. Maybe we will. WARNING: You will cry.

"The Sacred Hunt"

"Uncle Buddy!" my 10-year-old nephew shouted to me from the porch of his house as I stepped out of my car to attend his 10th birthday party. "Hurry up! I gotta show you my birthday present."

A couple minutes earlier as I drove up the long, gravel driveway to my sister's house in the beautiful countryside 20 miles outside the capitol city of Mississippi, I saw him outside in the yard with his best friend who was over for his party. The other boy was dressed for the cold. His mother had dropped him off for the whole day. My nephew wore only red, long-handle underwear and cowboy boots. He was poking at their newly started bonfire: Nephew was the keeper of the bonfire. Getting the fire going for their use the rest of the day for all sorts of drama was so important to him, he had not stopped long enough to put on outer clothes, or coat, when the bonfire need arose.

My nephew cracks me up. He has loved a bonfire ever since he was a small child. I joke to the family he is like a legal, bonfire pyromaniac. He loves it when land is cleared, resulting in a big pile of trees and brush that must be burned.

When I saw him as I came up the drive, he reminded me of a skinny cowboy who had been in the outhouse without his guns when an early morning gunfight erupted and he had been caught out in the open. I had laughed aloud in my car as he saw me and broke for the house, running in his cowboy boots, like somebody named *Slim*, or *Jesse*, as if a tornado was just over the tree line.

By the time I pulled up and shut off the car, he was on the porch, waving at me.

"Uncle Buddy, hurry! I gotta show you my birthday present."

"I'm coming, I'm coming," I said to him, dimly remembering how it was when I was so young and could get so excited about boy things that I thought I would literally pop.

I made it just inside the kitchen door. He held his present out as if for military inspection, "See, see," he said, "it's a .243 with a scope," as though I couldn't see the big, black, telescopic device, with its impressive glass at each end, the standard sized thing, setting atop the youth, single shot rifle like a mat-black tennis ball can.

"*Deddy* and I are going huntin' before it gets dark," he said. I pushed the button on the right side of the top of the rifle just before the beginning of the stock and in the natural place the right-handed shooter's thumb rests beside the hammer. The whole barrel of the rifle dropped down like it was designed to do, revealing where the shooter is to put the cartridge in the barrel before closing to fire.

I opened the kitchen door and stepped onto the porch. I looked through the scope, down the long drive way from where I had come and where, only 5 minutes earlier, 3 deer crossed in front of my car, one of them seeming as long as the butane tanks many people in the county have behind their houses for heating fuel storage.

"Here's the bullet Uncle Buddy," he said, pulling one of the shiny, new cartridges out of the brand new box and pushing it at me. "Uncle Buddy," he asked with 10 year-old, squeaky voice, "do you think this gun kicks as much as the 30-30?"

"No," I said. "The .243 kicks much less, the bullet is smaller. See it," I said, pointing to the projectile part of the cartridge. "It's only point 2-4-3," I said, "hence, the name," I continued, trying to promote better vocabulary and grammar to my nephew, without saying I was doing so.

"You have not shot your new gun?" I asked.

"No, not yet," he said, "I just got it this morning."

"Oh," I said. "Hey," I continued, "will you show me your and your daddy's deer stand like you said you would?" I asked him as he stood there in his red long johns and heavy socks, holding his new gun as if it were Christmas morning. But, it was his birthday, December 6.

He ran to his room like the world was ending and we had to hurry up and see the deer stand before it was all over. He came out wearing a tan, insulated jump suit that was too big. He looked like he rattled around in it. He had thick gloves in one hand, a dark gray ski mask in the other.

He bolted out the door and his friend followed. I fell in behind them.

They made a beeline for the old, red 4-wheeler. "Hey, Uncle Buddy, come on," he said, "we can all ride the 4-wheeler. You sit on the rack," he said as he jumped on it and his friend followed.

I said, "I want to walk for the exercise. It's not far; we have time before we have to be in for the party."

"You don't want to ride?" he said with a puzzled look on his face. He has always loved to drive, ride, or be a passenger in any mechanized vehicle, ever since he was a child.

He had been only two years old when we noticed that when he rode on the tractor in my father's lap, his grandfather— *Papa* as he called him, as in Papa Hemingway –he would lean forward in Papa's lap and turn the steering wheel of the tractor and simultaneously lean to one side and watch the corresponding turning of the front tires. He understood the correlation, even at only two years of age.

He called my mother, "Nannie." He was driving her golf cart around 8 acres of land as soon as he could reach the pedal and the steering wheel at the same time, which happened at its earliest when he could not yet sit on the seat and drive, but stood in front of the seat, leaned and forced back by the steering wheel, holding on to it as a manner of driving and using it to keep himself in front of the pedals.

When he was two and a half, he could back up his plastic, battery-powered John Deere™ Gator and parallel park it in just two, professional-looking moves under Papa's garage, in the midst of numerous, other mechanized toys he kept at Nannie's and Papa's.

So, over the thump of the cold, Honda motor, I asked him as I pointed to the horse corral approximately 200 yards away, "Where is the deer stand? Don't I walk down there and take a left at the horse corral?"

"Yessir," he said as he gunned the Honda and they took off, followed by his pack of big, pet dogs and their one, tiny, white poodle with pink toenails and pink bow on her head. I laughed but could not be heard over the Honda as they tore away, him looking like a bank robber in his ski mask, driving the get away vehicle and his friend, the same age as he, holding on and laughing as mud flew up behind them.

Papa pastors a nearby, country church. He is also a trained artist. A fine painter.

Papa being an artist and talking about Norman Rockwell pictures as I grew up, and my having seen prints of them all and an original in New England one time, my nephew and his friend and all the dogs reminded me of the Rockwell picture of the boys and their dog as they are running away with their clothes in hand from the posted swimming hole, obviously having been caught and rebuked by the landowner, who is pursuing them from outside the frame of the picture.

My nephew and his friend left me. It became quieter and I watched my boots as they landed in the gravel and mud. I listened to the crunch. The sound was crisp in the cold, December air.

I made it to the horse corral, empty now as my sister had buried her old faithful horse who died of old age. She had sold all the other horses, one by one over the previous year, because she had lost her taste for the horse life, and had tired of the expense of feed since she no longer loved horses in the same way, anymore.

I turned left and started following the smaller road cut through the woods that led down to, somewhere, the big, infamous, 2-man deer stand, from which, it was decided, my nephew was to take his first deer, under the supervision of his father. I could hear the Honda in the distance. Then, I did not hear it, anymore.

I watched my boots come down on the wet road as I was being careful where I stepped because it was muddy in spots. I noticed the color of the soil, and it made me think of all the soil and the different colors of it I had walked, hunting and not hunting, in my 45 years of living, and at the times I was taking notice where I stepped.

I thought of Lowndes County, Mississippi where I went on my first, formal deer hunt. I was probably ten years old like my nephew. I remembered that back then, before Thinsulate and Gore-Tex, I had worn green, rubber boots with yellow laces and a yellow band around the top edge because they were the thing to keep you dry, but I remembered that they were not very effective against the cold, even with bulky, wool socks. I remembered my feet being so cold in the rain that I thought they were going to fall off. And, I vaguely remembered, for a fleeting second, what it felt like to be a boy, and how I was scared I really would kill a deer, but I did not tell anyone, not even my daddy. I remembered the men ran dogs, which was new to me and so I did exactly what I was told, and that I was in my designated place and a deer came out 100 yards down the logging road I was sitting over, and I saw her, but I could not believe it because even seeing a deer was rare back then, and she was gone before I could react. I also recalled that later, someone asked me in front of a crowd of men, why I did not shoot. I had been embarrassed and could not answer. I just stood there, freezing in my green, rubber boots.

I thought about Rodney, Mississippi, a ghost of a town with a rich history back there, somewhere, and the cannon ball, still in the wall of the church, a thousand yards from Old Man River, across what seemed to be largest field in the world, and where in the steep hills above the giant field, I had run down the finger of a ridge and the big, big buck was running another, parallel ridge for a time, and due to turns in both ridges that went my way and cut down my distance, I had beaten him to their natural intersection.

I was standing there when he came out, his antlers looking like a big, white, perfectly symmetrical, mature, oak branches, and I remembered how we looked each other in the eyes, and that time had frozen for a split second. I remembered I stood there with my rifle up and ready and he in the cross-hairs of my scope, and that I had known I had him, and that had been enough. I had let him pass.

The occasion of my nephew's 10-year birthday and his guileless fascination with the simple, boyhood things, made me realize I am older, now.

I thought about all the other places I had walked. I thought about Spain and the dry soil in the arid climate, and how I had grown to love it.

I remembered walking out over the dusty ground and up the side of a hill amongst an olive grove in Portugal, and how the olive trees and their produce were interesting to me, a native Mississippian.

I remembered the red dirt in Arizona I walked over for miles that turned my boots red, to that place where the vortex of energy is located, the place to which people like to go to on pilgrimage, thinking the energy is good for them in mysterious ways. It might be. I do not claim to know.

I remembered Colorado and walking up that mountain and the foliage I found at different altitudes, and a storm coming in quickly, and it scaring me because it made me feel small in comparison to my surroundings, and to the power of the storm which, due to my altitude and exposure, seemed to pour directly from the throne of God.

I walked up on the Honda parked to the left in a little finger of a pine thicket. It was quiet. I stood there for a minute, listening for the two boys, envious of their rapture into the small adventure.

They screamed and jumped out of the woods on my right, laughing, nephew's friend saying they should have waited a minute longer, let me pass, then, jumped out from behind me. "That would have scared him," he said to my nephew. He agreed, and they patted backs, caught up in their 10-year-old-boy conspiracy.

Nephew had learned from his father to park the four-wheeler away from the stand to minimize noise, human scent, and the odors from the molecules of gasoline, oil, and from the mechanical thing itself.

We walked together and I listened as they talked about what they knew of hunting and other things. I remembered, slightly, about being a boy, and always striving to be in possession of some morsel of boyhood truth, information like according to my nephew's friend, if a doe and a fawn come out on you and the fawn has spots, you may *not* shoot the doe; but, if the fawn has outgrown his or her spots, you may shoot the doe. I did not remember because I had not been confronted with that conundrum for some time, but I suspected he was right, and I thought even if right or wrong, it was a good maxim to hunt by, and that I would have followed it if I hunted that day. And, maybe I would follow it, forever.

We arrived at the stand. It was over a small clearing about 100 yards long, 75 yards wide in front, and skewed to the left. There were no stumps.

Behind the stand, there was a barbed wire fence running out of sight to the right. On the other side of the fence, there was a large pasture. But, I saw no cows in it. When sitting in the stand, there was a lane cut down the fence row as for a pipeline, but no pipeline. The lane was approximately 25 yards wide, and ran parallel with the fence. It and the fence went out of sight. It would present, I thought to myself, the opportunity to catch deer as they moved into it to cross the fence into the field, or as they funneled down the fence-line and crossed when they decided to do so in order to go into the forest.

There was a clear shot for as far as one could shoot up the lane that ran parallel to the fence. *So to hunt from this stand,* I thought as I looked the situation over, *you might get your shot close in or far away in the lane to the right, or you more likely would get your shot in the small field right there in your lap, in front of you, and any shot in the field would be no greater than 100 yards.*

My nephew was talking as if he were a color commentator at the Super Bowl. He has always been a talker. We joke he talks like a girl, just riding down the road, he talks. Sometimes you have to ask him to give it a rest.

They asked me to watch them and they climbed the ladder to the stand and had a seat. It was a big, 2-man, lean-to stand, bolted securely to the oak tree by my nephew's daddy. He is a firefighter with big, strong, arms and hands, who knows how to use come-a longs, chains and other such equipment. I had no doubt about the security of the stand.

My nephew pointed out where the deer had been he missed a week earlier. "He was right there where that stick is in the ground," he said. "I would'a got him if I had my .243. Yep. But, all I had was my .410, and all it has for a site is a bead on top of the barrel."

I listened as I leaned my head back and watched them up there in the stand.

"Did you have buck shot, or a slug?" I asked.

"Buck shot," he called down.

"That's kinda a long shot. I understand how a fella could miss that," I said, faintly remembering how I felt when I had not even shot at the doe that came out on that logging road, and wanting to keep his confidence in tact, especially in front of his friend.

His mother, my sister, had already told me his daddy, who had been with him when he shot and missed, told her my nephew had completely lost his cool and was shaking like a leaf in a thunderstorm. I figured to myself he might have even shot the small shotgun off in a miss, on purpose, as a quarterback throws out of bounds. Shooting away would be better than a total freeze up, at least you could blame it on the gun or some other exogenous factor that would give you plausible deniability and allow you to save face.

They came down and we walked back to the 4-wheeler. I listened to more pontificated, 10-year-old-boy-wisdom. I was happy and thankful I was there with them. I found myself profoundly thrilled they were still innocent and living in wonderment of the simplest things.

Nephew called me the next morning, Sunday. "Uncle Buddy, you coming out after church?"

"I don't know," I said. "Did you and your daddy go hunting late yesterday after I left?"

"No," he said. "*Deddy* had to go to the fire station. Do you want to go hunting this afternoon before Papa's church tonight?"

"Man, I don't know. What if we get one?" I said. "We might miss church because of it, and Papa wouldn't like that. He'd be right, you know."

I went to Papa's house for lunch. It is just down the road from my sister's house.

My nephew called about 1:30. He wanted me to come down and we take his new gun and walk down and hunt from the stand for a little while. I had my hunting bag in the trunk of my car. I wish I had not because without it, I would have had a real excuse.

I could have lied for the greater good. I gave in.

He drove the Honda and I rode behind him down to the finger in the pines. It was dead quiet, cold, and there was no breeze.

This made me uneasy because the conditions were perfect. I knew the fact was, that being in this part of Hinds County, we would likely see deer, close up, and I knew if he put the scope's cross-hairs on one, his new .243 would coldly do its job.

I knew he did not yet realize the definite nature of such a rifle, with such a scope.

During the short ride on the Honda, I had thought back about the first deer I'd taken with a Winchester 30-30 I still possess. I was much older than he, in fact I was an adult, and even being older, I recollected on the back of the Honda how it had given me pause, that it had made me feel uneasy as I walked up to him, a youthful, regal, 8-point buck, and how I had realized at that moment how sacred a thing it was aside from all the manly talk.

I remembered I immediately figured out new things about life and death through mysterious pathways like it had come over the air from Indians long gone, and that later I read what I had felt and learned *my* own day from men who had learned and knew before me on *their* day, and who were writers and wanted to write about it to make sure fair chase rules were followed for generations to come. I remembered about that uneasy and reverent feeling I had the first time, and every time, that washes over you when you walk up to your quarry, and I remembered it being similar but not exactly the same as you feel at a funeral home wearing suit and tie when a human dies and you are visiting with the family.

This, I thought, *should be something he experiences with his daddy.* But, I could not figure out at that time how I could get out of it, and it did not occur to me just to tell him no, that there was something about it he'd understand later, and that he needed to wait for his father.

He thinks this is a fun outing, and it is, I thought, *but a deer is going to come out on us, crap!, and he is going to shoot him, and the deer is going to drop, and I have to be ready for that, including cleaning the deer by myself because it will probably rattle him, and I have to get all this done before 6 PM, not to mention I have to manage and maximize the hallowed nature of this whole life and death thing.*

I prayed a deer would not come out, not that day, even while on the other hand I hoped one would. I apologized to the Lord for praying with a forked tongue. Finally, I said to Him it was in His hands for the greater good, and that I knew He would know any and all greater good in the situation, if it existed. It was a cop out, I know, but I told myself I was doing the best I could.

Sometimes when you go hunting, you know you are going to be

successful. It is a gut feeling. I had it.

I did not know what his dad had gone over with him, or what he had not. I had to cover the basics.

Before we walked away from the four-wheeler, I turned him around by his skinny little shoulders in his bulky, insulated jumpsuit and I bent down to get eye level with him. "Ok," I whispered, "look here, these conditions are almost perfect. We are going to slip down there making as little noise as possible. We are going to climb that stand, you first, and we are going to be seated and sit there, very still. The stand is open. So, it is going to be cold, and we have to be still, very, very, still because the stand is exposed and we can be seen more easily than if we were in a covered box stand, you know?"

"Yessir," he whispered back.

I continued. "When we're in the stand, don't move your head too fast, move your eyes first, and then your head to follow, really slowly. Deer can see you move from Memphis, you know what I mean?"

"Yessir."

"Ok, when he or she comes out, they likely will not have seen us, if we were still. Let him get settled in that little opening, let him eat and all, then slowly, and I mean slowly, preferably when his head and eyes are down or away from us, pull your gun up to position, breath, relax, and when you get ready to shoot, take a breath and let half of it out, and then sqeeeeeeeeze the trigger. Put the cross-hairs just a hair behind his front shoulder. Got it?"

"Yessir. You think we're gonna get one?"

"I think yes," I said. "Yep, I do. I got a feeling."

I looked at him. He had that look in his eye I probably had when I was his age. I was not going to let him down.

We walked back to the stand and as we went, I showed him how to walk quietly. He did it well.

We arrived. I looked at my watch. It was 2:30 PM.

I tied a thin rope to his rifle and handed him the empty end. He climbed the ladder and sat down. I climbed the ladder with my rifle slung over my shoulder. No cartridge in chamber.

I sat and helped him retrieve his rifle. I tried to think of it all. I was not used to hunting with a boy, or doubling in a stand with anyone for that matter. I was adapting as I went.

I motioned him to lean over toward me and I whispered in his ear, "Ok, we're gonna be still and see what develops. I think the deer will likely come out of those woods straight in front of us to get to this grass, or he or she might walk down the road we walked in on, you know we saw all those tracks. I will watch to our right since I'm on the right side, you don't worry about it over here, you watch in front; watch the field, and pay attention to the spot the road comes into the field. You want to see 'em before they see you. The deer will appear out of the blue, like a ghost." He shook his head; he had heard his father and me talk about how deer would, all of a sudden be there, and that we would never get over that for as long as we lived. "Let's be still and quiet," I finished.

He looked back and up at me with big, brown eyes. He nodded his ski-masked covered head.

"Put a bullet in your gun," I said. His eyes widened. He shook his bank robber head, again. He turned back, pushed the button, broke the barrel down, put in the shiny, deadly, cartridge, and closed the barrel back with a tiny 'click.' I could see his little fingers where slightly shaking.

"Safety on?" I asked.

He checked. Then, turned again and looked at me with his big, brown eyes, shining with youth. He shook his head.

I leaned over and whispered, "One more thing: when the deer comes you want to shoot, be careful you take the safety off quietly so it won't click."

He looked at me again and winked one of his big eyes.

Thus began our sitting there 15 feet in the air, looking down on Mississippi forestland displaying the last colors of fall. It was calm, but when the wind did stir, the leaves quivered in the trees, blurring the hues as if on the canvas of an Impressionist.

The view was spectacular, like sharp, bucolic photos, the colors made even more vivid by a traveling mercy I had not calculated: That we had the sun behind us in the West, pleasantly shining into our small field, and warming the backs of our necks like the heater of God against the surrounding cold.

When I realized the position of the sun, I realized that if the deer did come out of the forest in front of us, or from down the lane we walked in on in front and coming into our little field, right to left, the sun would be in the deer's face, and that would be good, except we would have to be extra careful about any unnatural movement of our silhouettes.

I thought about whether to say anything. I decided I should, partly as a precaution, and because it had become my responsibility to do on-the-job-training about the whole experience, to the extent I understood it myself.

I touched him on his hand. I leaned over, and keeping his eyes out front and watching with impressive vigilance, he put the right side of his ski mask where his ear was located to me.

I thought about the thing I had to communicate and how to make the point quickly, and understandably.

"Notice," I said like I was talking to an adult because I wanted to do my part, the best I could, to instruct him to be a good communicator, "when the deer comes in from the front, even from down that lane we walked, the sun is in the West behind us, and it will be in his or her face, that is good, except think about it: We must be extra careful about how we move because our silhouette will be very easy to see, like an unnatural clump up in this tree, and he could see us, and be spooked, and be gone before you get a chance." He did not look at me, but he shook his ski mask.

I was glad I said something then because it was my job to do so, and his vigilance confirmed he had stepped up into the situation and was ready, at least to the point of a deer coming out: *we'll see how we cross that bridge when a deer comes out*, I thought.

I looked at my watch at approximately 3:05. At that moment, I had an immense feeling of understanding come over me like the Holy Spirit washed over the people at Pentecost.

At approximately 3:08, two, big doe materialized in the edge of the field like deer often do, as if ghosts, even though they had walked down the lane we walked to the lush grass of our opening.

My nephew was sitting forward in his seat when they appeared. I leaned up slowly and positioned my mouth behind his ear. "Ok," I whispered more softly than before, "hang on, let it get right, and we'll get your gun up."

He did not move his head, but I knew he heard. I stayed in position behind his ear.

The doe turned their necks around and looked back up the lane. "Slowly get your gun up and rest it on the bar and hang on till they get all the way in the field: they don't know we're here; the wind is blowing across our faces and out to our right; we have a small window here to get this done."
He slowly put the gun up and rested it on the bar that was part of the stand and went across in front of us like a bar you pull into yourself on a roller coaster, but it was much thinner, made of aluminum tubing, stationary, and padded.

I whispered, "Let the doe come on out but don't shoot yet, I think there is a buck behind them, must be in rut, they keep looking back and are agitated; if they come out right, he will follow exactly where they stepped because of their scent, even if they turn, and when he does, and if he is good, he's your deer; this won't take long; pull the hammer back, now, and hang on, we'll say when to shoot."

I said 'we'll say when to shoot' instead of 'I'll say when to shoot' so that he would feel in on the decision, so his confidence would be built, so he would have a good story for his friends. I could hear him even then say to the other boys, "he came out and I decided he was my deer and I shot, and…"

I was amazed and thankful at my own lucidity in the moment. I realized it was beyond me, that it must be grace; grace granted for this sacred slice of time with my nephew, the impressionable boy.

The does' tails stayed down but constantly twitched, and they kept looking back up the thin road. They moved on into the field and looked back, again. I felt my heart beating in my throat.

At 3:11, the buck quickly materialized but was partially obscured by a big, southern pine in the opening of the narrow road to our small coliseum. He had his nose to the ground, following the scent of the doe, even though he could look up and see them in the open, a mere 20 yards ahead. I knew the window of time for our shot might be tight, depending on what the doe were about to do. My heart beat loudly in my ears but I felt strangely calm because the boy was depending on me and I had a job of eternal importance to do.

"Watch the does," I whispered, "'as they go, he goes,' get ready; when he takes one more step and clears the pine, take him!" I slowly sat back. There was nothing else I could do.

I could see part of the buck's neck. It was uniformly swollen and reminded me, for some reason, of a heating and air conditioning duct. I got intermittent glimpses at his eyes that were so crazed by passion, you could see them from where we were-- they were stretched, wildly. He had taken leave of all his senses that keep him safe in the forest during all other times of the year except this time-- the rut --when the circle of life drives him, the other bucks, and all the does, to make continuation of their species certain, until the fullness of time.

I knew we would likely have one second, one solid second, when the buck was still and the ethical shot could be made. I prayed for my nephew that he could hold and deliver at the appointed moment.

For me, everything went into slow motion and fell dead quiet. The buck took one step and cleared the pine. Right then, it was as if God put him there as He had put the ram in the bush for Abraham. The buck raised his head and sniffed the air; the does were looking back at him; he put his nose back to the ground and was about to start his charge of nature, again, and the .243 discharged. I heard it faintly, like it was a mile away; everything was so slowed down, I felt like I could almost see the bullet as it traveled its 3900 feet per second. I saw the buck's eyes in surprise as the smooth, spinning projectile hit him. Hair puffed out of him on the other side like when a child blows a dandelion in a field on a sunny, summer day. The buck died right there on his feet, and he collapsed to the ground as though a trap door had fallen out from under him, but he did not fall into the earth.

I felt myself collapse from being tautly wound. I instinctively reached around my nephew's neck with my left arm and grabbed the rifle as he folded and slumped over into me and I held the gun out behind him. I turned and hugged him into me with my right arm, and I could feel his thin, skeletal frame inside the big jumpsuit release into me, in resolution. I held us up.

It was deadly calm. I sat there for about 15 seconds, holding him up and looking out to the buck lying peacefully in the grass. My nephew felt as limp as a dishrag.

"Ok, you Ok?" I said as I pushed him up.

He leaned up and looked at me though his ski mask. He was holding on to the bar with one hand and to my arm with the other. He was quivering. "Yessir," was all he could say.

"There he lies out there," I said. "You did it." I nodded my head toward and pointed to the field and his buck.

He still did not look. "Yessir, Uncle Buddy," he said.

I realized that as taking animals from the wild goes, he could not yet speak because the sacred nature of what he had just done was washing over him and he did not want to look upon his quarry until his attitude, until his spirit, was right. So, I leaned back against the tree and let it be what it was for the time it needed to be.

He dropped his head and sat there. After the appropriate time, probably 30 seconds, he raised his head and looked out to the field and upon his buck. The sun was coming in from the West even lower now and it lit the contrasts of the colors of the buck against the grass. His antlers were light in color. They stood out against the other hues around us on the canvas of our little stadium, framed by the trees and the blue, Mississippi sky.

I knew what he was likely thinking. "He's a 4 point," I said, "unless he has brow tines you can hang a wedding band on, then he's a 6, but I think he's a good 4, shoot, a great 4. He's young and very handsome," I said, me being a fiction writer and suddenly inspired that Hemingway would have described him that way, "but he's big; did you have time to notice? He's probably 170 lbs or so."

He still did not say anything, and he was visibly shaking as I had done the morning I took my first deer, which was a very nice 8 point over in Alabama on the Tombigbee River the morning after we had eaten at a fish camp restaurant on the opposite side of the river from our cabin. The restaurant was on the literal edge of the cold, slow river. Its timbered exterior and inside looked frozen in time, with hundreds of game mounts of many species on the log walls. I remembered it felt as if Teddy Roosevelt might walk in, and that while we ate hot catfish fillets, I could see a big light, like a ghost, coming up the river. The light was on the bridge of a tug boat as it pushed a barge as long as a football field by the restaurant, very slowly, and in the thick darkness, so thick you could barely see the barge as the tug pushed it by at a crawl as though they were in a funeral procession. I recalled that as they got even with us and passed, you could see them only in ghostly silhouette but you knew they were there because the huge light floated above them, suspended, as it were, in the impenetrable blackness, punching a hole in the dead, dead, dark ahead, swinging back and forth, back and forth, lighting the edges of the river for the pilot.

"Ok," I said to my nephew, "we have to move out, you ready?"

"Yessir," he said.

I tied his rifle to the rope and I went down. He let his rifle down and he came down behind it.

It had been long enough. I knew the buck was dead. But, I felt like it was my responsibility to demonstrate how to approach.

"Look," I turned and said, "let's put a bullet in your gun and approach this deer like we are supposed to, Ok?"

He fumbled for a cartridge like Barney Fife, put it in the barrel, and shut it with a good 'click.'

"Get up beside me," I said. My gun was loaded, too, with one in the chamber. "You walk up beside me and watch what I do."

We arrived at the buck from behind him. I reached out with the barrel of my rifle and punched him in his upside hindquarter. He did not move. He was dead.

"Ok, take your cartridge out, now," I said. He did, and I unloaded my gun, too. "Why don't you take your ski mask off," I said.

I knelt down at the head of his deer and motioned him to come along beside me. I patted the deer and rubbed his smooth coat, with the grain. He did the same.

"Look at his antlers, Uncle Buddy," he said.

I picked one side up in each hand and held his head up. "Get in front and take a look at him," I said. He did.

"Wow," he said, "he's pretty."

"Hemingway would say he's handsome," I said. "You ever read Hemingway's stories about hunting?"

"No sir," he said.

"Maybe I'll have to give you that for Christmas," I said. "Speaking of books," I said pulling out the little Fair Chase book I had for 15 years, and that I brought with me in case we took a deer, in order to teach the gravity of the situation. "When I killed, or when I took my first deer I should say, I felt funny, funny like I was a little upset but in a good way, and it had to do with my knowing, almost out of nowhere, that while it was Ok to take him, it was also a serious matter, and I should acknowledge that and respect it."

He shook his head. I had done what I thought I should do, and it had been the right thing: I had talked first and confessed, in my own words, what he was feeling, what all good and ethical hunters feel every time they take an animal from the wild.

"Listen to this." I said as I opened the little book and read, "If there is a sacred moment in the ethical pursuit of game, it is the moment you release the arrow or touch of the fatal shot."

I followed up. "You took this nice buck with a good shot when you were supposed to and he died immediately. That is how it is supposed to be, every time. Don't take a chancy shot, take the good one, or do not take one at all."

He shook his head, his eyes as big as saucers.

"Listen to this," I said as I read more: "If there is a time for reverence in the ethical hunt, it is when you claim, or accept, what you have killed."

"That's what we are doing now," I said. "The little book goes on to say that what we have before us is a wild animal, and he is a product of many things, and this is the appropriate time to pause and appreciate what has taken place here today. I'm telling you, I know how you feel because I felt the same way, and you should feel the same way every time, and the day you don't, stop hunting."

He shook his head. Tears were welled up in his eyes because he had crossed the Rubicon, as it were, and now he understood mysterious things like from the Indians and it moved him in ways he had not been moved in his 10 years. I walked over, and standing over the buck, I hugged him, and he hugged me back.

I took out my sister's small, digital camera I had taken off the kitchen table before we left his house. "Why don't you squat behind your buck's head and hold his head up by the antlers, in the classic way, and let me take your picture."

"Ok," he said. He was a little skittish, but he succeeded, and I took three pictures from slightly different angles. Two were good. The flash lit him and the deer. And, the light coming in from the western sky lit the backdrop, including the beautiful colors of the Mississippi forest.

On the way to get the 4 wheeler, I thought about how it would not be long before he would be taller than me like his daddy. I put my arm around his shoulders and he put his around my waist and I patted him and hugged him to me, briefly, and let him go because 10 year old boys do not want to hug too long.

We were very close to home and the skinning rack and it was cold out, so I did not have to field dress the buck.

We got the deer to the house and my sister and my little narrow, 6 year-old niece came out with her eyes as wide as her ear muffs were large. Nannie and Papa came up from their house. We took pictures and I stuck my finger in a little of the buck's blood and smeared it on my nephew's face, but only about as much as football players' black under their eyes to fight glare. And, I added a close-up picture of him with the blood on his face to the portfolio of the hunt, for posterity.

We hung the buck, I opened him up, Papa helped us make the appropriate cuts, and his entrails fell out into the big washtub. We did not have much time before having to be at Papa's church but I felt compelled, as I had throughout the day, to set as good an example for him as I possibly could. I took the little book out of my pocket again and handed it to Papa and he said, "My hands are bloody," and I said it was Ok, that I had already stained the book, and it was the right thing to do.

Papa, my nephew, and I stood next to the buck and it felt like we were at a graveside, funeral service, and Papa, ever the Pastor-teacher, said, "And now a thing we think of at this time. The book reads:

'Field dressing begins the natural process that involves scavenging birds, insects, and decay as the unused parts return to the energy and nutrient cycles of the ecosystem. This is a marvelous process of renewal, and surplus parts of what you harvest should be thoughtfully returned to the earth.'"

Papa closed the book and handed it back to me.

"Therefore," I said looking at and speaking to my nephew, "we are going to put this washtub full of the entrails of this buck we've taken today and return him to the earth for the benefit of all other animals dependent on him for continuation."

We put the tub on the back and he fired up the 4 wheeler. I rode back with him to the spot where the deer died, where the grass was still pressed down from the weight of his body. I told my nephew it was probably not mandatory we put the entrails right in this exact spot but if you could, it was good, and since we could, we should, and he understood and shook his head. We dumped the tub and stood there for several seconds. While we were standing there, I looked up at the stand and looked back down at him, "That was an excellent shot," I said.

He replied, "Yea, that *was* pretty good wasn't it, Uncle Buddy?"

Before we climbed back on the 4-wheeler, I said, "Here, this is yours, now," extending the little book. "Read it, use it, and pass it along one day when you know it is time. This has been a sacred hunt."

We made it to Papa's church. My mother, sister, niece, nephew and

I sat together. I sat beside my nephew and I could still smell the iron-like scent of blood. I whispered to him about it and he said he could smell it, too.

Papa took the podium. He deviated from his planned topic, and told of what had taken place that day.

Then, he talked about blood, and that the deer and the goat were of the same family. And, that the Book says the blood of goats and calves were not sufficient for us to enter into the Holy place. Then, Papa told of *The* blood, and I looked at my nephew and winked and he winked back because we knew of that blood about which Papa spoke because we had believed, he one day with Papa in the cab of Papa's old, little, red, Chevy Luv truck in Papa's pecan orchard as they tended a bonfire made of limbs they cut, when he had asked Papa what must a 'little boy' do to be saved?

I happened to be at my sister's house the next weekend and in earshot of my nephew and two of his friends. I listened with immense pleasure as he told of the hunt, and that he did so in detail and with reverence, and that one of his friends who had not yet taken a deer asked, *How many times did you shoot him?*, and that my nephew responded, "Oh, once, I shot him once, and it was what you call the ethical shot; and, we took his guts back out to the other animals so we can go hunting again when we need to."

"Entrails," I said to him across the room, "Not guts, entrails," and I smiled and winked.

"Yessir," he said to me as he turned to his friends, "entrails, that's what you're supposed to say, entrails."

"Entrails," one of the boys said, "I never heard that."

"Oh yea," my nephew said with a tone of wisdom, "that's what a good hunter calls them. That's what the little book says."

I was home in my bed. Loved ones and friends, younger and old, were coming over to see me and to say good-bye.

Our wonderful Nannie and Papa had been gone for years. So had my beloved wife.

My only sibling, my younger sister, was there in the kitchen, managing the food and dishes and talking with visitors.

Today was my day to die. I knew it. It was Ok.

My nephew came into my room. There were big tears in his eyes like there had been over 40 years ago as we stood over his first buck below that double deer stand.

"Hey Uncle Buddy," he said.

"Hey, man," I said. "I think today's the day," I said to break the ice and to put him at ease.

"Don't say that," he said, "I don't want you to go."

"Son," I said, "it is Ok. I am almost 90 and I've had a great life. I'm ready to go. I have no reservations whatsoever. The way I look at it, I get to see my wife again, and I get to see Nannie and Papa before you do. We'll be there when you get there."

He started crying, a man 50 years old now, but he loved me and I him, the son I never had. He cried slowly, softly, and constantly, his tears rolling down his cheek and landing on his shirt and the bed covers as he sat at the foot of my bed. He got up and came over and hugged me and cried into my neck and I patted him and told him I loved him. He told me he loved me, and he said, "Thank you."

I didn't know or ask him for what, but I said "Ok."

He sat up. "I want to show you something," he said. He opened a soft case he brought in and pulled out the little book I had given him in the field that day, forty years before, when he had taken his first deer. "It still has your fingerprints made from the blood of that 4-point buck I took that day with you right there by my side in that two-man stand."

He handed me the book. I held it and looked at my bloody fingerprints on the cover. I opened it up to the pages Papa had read before we took the entrails away.

There, were the fingerprints of Papa; and, I remembered him, my daddy, standing there with us. I could hardly believe it because it had been so long ago. But, I remembered him standing in the pulpit later that night and what he talked about, and I started to cry, and I was happy on my deathbed because I knew that before that day was over, I would see my father, my *Deddy*, again, and he would hug me and it would be all right, and I said through the tears, "These are Papa's fingerprints, here."

My nephew took the book and looked at the page with Papa's fingerprints. He started to cry again like a soft rain, "I didn't know that," he said, "but they would be there because you handed him the book and he read, too."

"Just think, I'll see Papa in just a little while."

"I don't want you to go," he said, again.

"It is all right. It's time," I said.

He sat up, looked at me, and rubbed the side of my face with the palm of his hand like he was trying to sear how I looked that day into his mind so he would not forget. "I want you to do something for me," I said.

"Anything," he said.

"Get that box off the top shelf in the closet and bring it here." He brought it to the bed and set it beside me.

"I've been very fortunate in my life," I said. I've had 30 books published."

"I did not know it was 30," he said.

"Yes, 30, and I started late," I said. "In this box, are 2 copies of number 31. I want you to open it next week and send one of the two manuscripts in here to my publisher. Keep the other for a copy. I signed it in blue ink at the end. It might be worth something to you later because it is signed. The cover letter and address and everything are on top. The publisher is expecting it next week. They have read part of it. My agent has already made the deal, including the marketing plan. Royalties will go to the family, including you."

My nephew left late in the afternoon, telling me he would be back the next day.

That night at about 11 PM, I woke up and the most peaceful feeling I had ever felt in my life swept over me. I laid there in the dark and I knew it was time. Everything starting turning light and increasingly white. I felt the purest love surround me like warm, swaddling clothes. It was out of this world, and without any terrestrial adulteration, whatsoever.

I thought of Papa, and of him saying, "Now comes Grace for dying."

The next week, my nephew went to my favorite shipping store and he and the owner, George, talked about me and how they missed me. George, asked him what he wanted to ship, and to where.

My nephew told him what I had said and they opened the box and looked in. On top as I had told him, was my letter to my publisher. They read it with interest because my body was now dead and gone, and in part of the letter, because I knew it was my time to go when I wrote it, I thanked my publisher for all they had done for my career, and me.

My nephew removed the cover letter of instruction. There, was the opening page of the top copy of the manuscript.

He looked at it, read the title and the opening paragraph. His mouth fell open.

George asked, "What's the matter?"

My nephew turned the box around for George to see. There, was the story I waited 40 years to write: <u>The Sacred Hunt</u>.

The story came out and swept the hunting world. I had prearranged the cover to display a hunting collage, including the two, good pictures I shot of him long ago: One of him in the field, holding the antlers of his fine buck; and, the other, the close up of his face, with streaks of blood under his big, brown, 10-year old eyes, and him smiling confidently after *our* sacred hunt in the wild, vivid woods of Mississippi.